The Showstopper
A Wing and a Prayer Mystery
ROBIN MERRILL

New Creation Publishing

Madison, Maine

Chapter 1

The candy apple red minivan veered off toward the trees, and Sandra flung her arm out to save the imaginary person in the front seat as she pumped the brakes. She had no idea whom she was trying to save. No one ever sat in the front passenger seat, except for the few times her angel friend had ridden around with her.

"What's happening?" Peter asked from the middle seat.

The van slid to a halt inches shy of the ditch, and Sandra lowered her arm as she eased the van back out onto the road. She didn't want to take the time to gather herself, because someone might rear-end them while she sat collecting her unwieldy emotions. The visibility was about ten feet.

"Dad says it doesn't do any good to pump the brakes."

Not appreciating the timing of his criticism, Sandra didn't respond until she was heading in the right direction and safely in her lane. At least, she *thought* she was in her lane. Even if she *could* see the lines on the road, this road didn't have any lines. Back road Mainers guessed where the lanes were. Tourists usually guessed wrong. "It's a habit. When I learned to drive, if we lost control of the vehicle, we pumped our brakes."

"'Cause those were old cars."

"Peter! Do you mind? I'm risking our lives for your burgeoning theater career here. I could do without the constant criticism."

"Sorry," he mumbled, and she believed him. He was probably just nervous about the weather, and this anxiety was manifesting as snark.

"I'm sorry too. I didn't mean to snap at you. I'm just so far beyond irritated that they're holding rehearsal tonight. I mean, are you kidding?" She leaned forward and peered upward. "Look at this! It's a blizzard!"

"Sorry."

She glanced into the rearview so she could look her almost-eleven-year-old in the eye. "The weather's not your fault, honey, and it's not your fault that they're having rehearsal in a blizzard. It's the director's fault." Yet she knew that she wouldn't say a word when they got there, *if* they got there. She wasn't good at confrontation. In fact, she tried to avoid it. Except when she was on the soccer field. She was getting pretty good at confrontation there.

But this wasn't soccer. This was *theater*, Peter's newest passion, though Sandra suspected he might be more interested in the young actress starring in the play than he was in the art form itself. Either way, Sandra had supported this new direction until tonight—until the blizzard. To be fair to the director, the revered Frank Flamatti, who had directed eight zillion plays in his sixty-year career, the forecast hadn't predicted this. And it hadn't even been snowing that hard when Sandra had left the house, or she might never have left it. But now they were winding their way up into the mountains, to this quaint little theater that should really stick to summer plays, to rehearse for the final play of the season: *The Homecoming: A Christmas Story*, a play based on the book *Spencer's Mountain*—the book that also inspired *The Waltons*.

Sandra had grown up watching reruns of *The Waltons*, and the show occupied a soft spot in her heart. She was thrilled that Peter had been cast as one of the Spencer brothers, so she tried not to be resentful of her immediate circumstances. The van slid again, but she regained control before they had a chance to panic.

"How much farther?" He was definitely worried.

"Not sure. It's hard to see any landmarks. I would say just a couple of miles? But don't be scared, honey. Your mom is an excellent driver." She started to hum *The Waltons* theme song.

"I'm not scared. But I'm still going to pray."

THE SHOWSTOPPER

Oh, duh. Why hadn't she prayed yet? "Good idea." She gave Peter a minute of silence to do his thing, and then she prayed aloud for the both of them and for everyone else headed toward Mountain View Theater.

When she'd said amen, Peter said, "We *do* need this rehearsal. I don't see how we can be ready in two weeks."

"I know, but I trust Mr. Flamatti. He knows what he's doing." Sandra forced her jaw to relax. She was too tense.

"I know, but some people don't even know their lines yet!"

She'd noticed. Someone called for their line nearly every other line. It drove her nuts. "They'll get there in time. Some people memorize faster than others."

"It's not that I'm fast at memorizing. It's that I worked hard at doing it."

"You're right. Sorry. I didn't mean to discount the time and work you've put in. But I'm sure they're working hard too."

Peter grunted his dissent with that cheery assessment, and she didn't blame him. There were a few of them who *hadn't* seemed to be working too hard, namely John Boy himself, who was originally called Clay Boy, but she couldn't help thinking of him as John Boy. A local college student, Matthew Longwood had gotten the role, but she didn't know how. He showed up late when he showed up at all, and didn't appear to be able to act his way out of a wet paper bag. He didn't seem the theater type. Or even the artist type. Or even the pleasant type. She suspected he'd only auditioned because Treasure Foss was staring in it—a woman, Sandra thought, far too sensual to be cast as Ma Walton, but what did she know? Treasure Foss on the bill probably sold more tickets.

"We should have offered Ethel a ride," Sandra muttered. When no one auditioned for Grandma Walton, Peter had encouraged Ethel to give it a shot, and she'd been a shoo-in. Sandra had been so proud of

3

him for thinking of Ethel, but then, all her kids were growing quite attached to their new cookie-baking babysitter.

"There!" Peter pointed, but Sandra couldn't see anything, her eyesight evidently inferior to his. But then she did see it, the outside light of the theater peeking through the white wall, and then the outline of the main building took shape.

"Thank God," she breathed out as she slowed to a crawl, not wanting to have to use the brakes before turning in.

"Um, there's no one here," Peter said.

Sandra scanned the parking lot and saw that he was right. There weren't nearly enough cars in the lot. She glanced at the clock. "We're only five minutes late, so others are probably even later. I'm sure we're not the only ones slowed by the storm. It was the same for everyone." She put the car in park, wishing she'd brought a shovel. She didn't know how much snow they were going to get, and she wasn't sure she'd be able to back out when rehearsal was over. Peter had started to open the door. "Hang on a sec, let me turn around while I still can, so I don't have to back out when we're done."

Peter groaned, but shut the door and leaned back in his seat.

She began her fifteen-point turn. Might as well pack the snow down while she was at it. "Maybe I'll ask Mr. Flamatti to let us go early—"

"No! Don't!"

"Honey, he'll understand."

"Then let someone else ask. I don't want to be the one."

"Fine." She put the car in park again. "Okay, let's go." They climbed out into the snow, and she turned her collar up against the large, fluffy flakes that were trying to sneak down her neck as she looked down to shield her eyes. Then she trotted for the closest door, grateful that she'd at least had the good sense to wear her boots. She sneaked a look at Peter's feet and was relieved to see that he too had worn boots.

Sometimes he tried to sneak out in flip-flops, even though it was December.

Peter beat her to the basement door and opened it for her, and she thanked him as she stepped into the warmth. At least the heat was on—for now. This area of the state was notorious for losing power. They didn't see anyone in the basement, so Peter headed up the narrow, rickety stairwell that led to the back of the theater. Sandra grabbed the handrail for support, but it wobbled so efficiently that it made her ascent more perilous, not less. She couldn't believe no one fixed these stairs. This theater must rake in serious cash from summer tourists, so they really could afford a new railing, but that obviously wasn't their priority. Till they got sued. Then it would become their priority.

I stand corrected. At the top of the stairs, the ledge was littered with tools: an electric drill with its cord hanging down like a bell cord; a bag of nails; a level that showed the ledge wasn't level at all; and a hammer. There were small kids in this play, and the placement of those tools was probably not ideal, but she tried to unsee it. She didn't want to spend the whole rehearsal worrying about safety, and this wasn't her barbecue.

Chapter 2

Sandra stepped out into the auditorium and saw a small group gathered in the front few rows. The director waved them over. Peter headed toward him, and Sandra headed for the back row to lay low.

"Would you come too, please?" Frank asked her in a formal tone. He was such a professional.

She changed course and went to sit beside Peter. Several years ago, the ancient theater had gotten a grant to get new chairs, and she was grateful for their comfort. She settled in and scanned the room to see who was there and was surprised to see that Ethel had indeed ventured out. That woman was fearless. Their eyes met, and Ethel gave her a springlike smile that clashed with their current circumstances. Sandra tried to return the smile, but knew hers didn't match Ethel's good cheer.

"I owe you all the most heartfelt apology," Frank began. "I've been here all day, and I've only just looked out the windows. I had no idea it was supposed to get this bad. As soon as I realized, I called as many people as I could and told them to stay home, but some of you were out of cell phone range." Sandra wasn't surprised. Thanks to the mountains, the theater had absolutely zero cell service. "Please accept my apologies. I hate that you've wasted a trip, but please do leave right now, in case it gets worse."

At first, no one said anything, and then Otis, who played a too-thin and not nearly jolly enough Grandpa Spencer, said, "But we're all here. We should rehearse!"

Frank shook his head. "I appreciate your enthusiasm, but I don't think that is wise. Your safety is my primary concern."

THE SHOWSTOPPER

Tell that to the hammer and drill.

"We're Mainers!" Otis cried. "We know how to drive in the snow. We're already here. We might as well take advantage—"

"A true Mainer knows when to stay off the roads," Billy offered.

Billy was starting to grow on Sandra. At first, his in-your-face friendliness had frightened her New England disposition, but the more she was around him, the more she appreciated him. Like now, for instance.

Otis folded his arms across his chest. "Well, I think we should stay." His tone suggested that he was now going to punish them all with the silent treatment.

"Maybe it could be optional?" Gloria offered. She wasn't an actress, but a chauffeur to her two thespian children, Corban and Corina. "We live nearby, so we could stay—"

"We could run Corban's and my scene!" Otis said, the silent treatment abruptly abandoned.

"It's up to you," Gloria said to Frank, her voice sounding meek and gentle compared to Otis's. "If you want to lock up and go home, then we should."

"Honestly, I've got so much work to do, I was just going to sleep here."

Otis slapped the arms of his chair. "It's settled then. If you want to go, go. If not, let's rehearse!"

"I've got a shovel!" Gloria said with too much excitement.

Sandra wasn't sure anything was settled, and she didn't like being forced into the decision-making hot seat. If she chose to go home, Peter would be mad, and they wouldn't be real Mainers. She didn't want to be the bad guy, but she really wanted to go home. But then she looked into Peter's giant doe eyes, which were pleading with her to stay. She nodded. "Fine. But you owe me."

His face lit up and he hurried to the stage, leaving her to reflect. Had she just agreed to stay to make Peter happy or because she feared the judgment of the others? Or both? She decided it didn't matter and picked up her knitting, which had gotten wet on the way into the theater. She wasn't much of a knitter, but she'd been spending so much time at the theater, everyone was getting a scarf for Christmas.

Jan, the stage manager, stood staring at the almost empty stage with her hands on her hips. "We've rehearsed in worse weather than this and lived to tell the tale," she said to no one. Jan had also been at Mountain View Theater for eons, and reminded people of this as often as possible.

The college student strolled in then, looking as though he'd just rolled out of bed. He brushed the snow off his gelled-solid hair and straightened his glasses. "It's snowing out. Why are we having rehearsal?"

No one acknowledged his existence, so he repeated his question with even more accusation in his tone. Treasure tossed him a look. "If you'd ever show up on time, you'd know. Now get in your place. You're in this scene."

"I'm in every scene," he mumbled as if that were a great oppression he was enduring, as if he'd never auditioned for such a role. He didn't go to his place. He crossed the stage to stand too closely to Treasure, who backed up a foot. Sandra couldn't blame her. Matthew's lips moved, but Sandra couldn't hear what he said. She had no problem, however, hearing Treasure's answer.

"I don't know how many times I have to tell you. I will never, ever, ever go out with you. So stop asking, you creep!" She stormed off the stage, and everyone watched her go. Sandra was certain that this was the way she wanted it. Sandra had never seen such an attention-seeking person in her life. Treasure wanted all eyes on her all the time, which made her a good actress. In a private conversation with Sandra, Billy had once called Treasure a "theater tramp," and Sandra had failed to bite back the laugh. The phrase fit. The single, twenty-something-year-old woman traveled all over the state to act in amateur plays. Sandra had no idea how she paid her bills, and had wondered why such a passionate actress hadn't moved to a place that offered paying roles. But Sandra didn't want to know badly enough to ask, so Treasure's motivation would have to remain a mystery.

Deciding she needed some caffeine, Sandra headed for the concession booth in the back of the theater. It wasn't open, but the cast and crew could help themselves and then drop their money into a can, on the honor system. Sandra had already stuck a twenty dollar bill in there, hoping that would cover all the Coke she could drink. As she passed the sound booth, she heard Otis say to Treasure, "Don't pretend to be such a victim. If you don't want him to like you, stop flirting with him."

"I don't flirt with him!" Treasure cried, as if Otis had accused her of drinking pond scum.

"You disgust me," Otis said and brushed by her, physically knocking her aside. As he did so, his eyes met Sandra's, and she quickly looked down to pretend she hadn't seen or heard anything.

Her cheeks got hot and she hurried to the fridge. Had that not been a bit aggressive? Treasure was obnoxious, sure, but she didn't deserve that! The more time Sandra spent with Otis, the less she liked him. However, she'd met his wife at other rehearsals, and she'd been lovely, so surely Otis must have some redeeming qualities?

Chapter 3

Not long after polishing off her Coke, Sandra had to use the ladies' room. Wanting to stretch her legs as much as possible and kill some time, she chose to use the downstairs one. As she passed the pile of tools at the top of the stairs, she thought about moving them, but decided against it. Most of the kids weren't here tonight, anyway. And it might be overstepping her bounds to start moving things around, even if her intentions were good. The soccer momming she had down, but she wasn't quite sure how to be a theater mom yet.

She met Gloria coming out of the bathroom and smiled at her. Now this woman was a *theater mom*. Her kids were in every Mountain View play that had kid parts. Maybe she should observe her more closely, try to get some pointers.

When Sandra came back out into the hallway, still wiping her hands on her jeans because there hadn't been any paper towels, she heard Treasure cackle in the green room and noted that she would make a fantastic Wicked Witch of the West if she could find a production of *The Wizard of Oz*. Though, she probably wouldn't take a role that didn't allow her to be beautiful. As it was, she was already insisting that Ma Walton get to wear bright red nail polish and her hair down.

"You're just a kid!" Treasure said. "You're not a real actress, and you never will be! You're not pretty enough!"

Sandra's blood boiled, and she flew toward the green room, almost smashing into Gloria, who beat her there. Sandra stopped in the doorway and surveyed the scene. Treasure was standing over poor little, adorable Corina, who was cowering beneath her pointed finger. What a load of bull! Corina was *gorgeous*. She had the perfect features for the stage: heart-shaped face; long, dirty-blond wavy hair; rosy cheeks; and pink lips. Sandra had no doubt that Corina would be beautiful for the rest of her life.

For a second, she feared that Gloria, in a full on mother's rage, was going to strike Treasure. She was shaking mad, and Sandra wondered if she should intervene just to protect Treasure. She didn't *want* to protect Treasure. She had come here to protect Corina, but she didn't want Gloria to go to jail for assault.

She took a tentative step forward, just in case.

"Don't you ever speak to my daughter like that." Gloria's words came out strong and staccato. Sandra made a mental note to never mess with Gloria or her children. Not that she ever would mess with anybody, but just in case.

Treasure leaned toward Gloria. "You're not scaring me, Mama Bear. I'm just trying to give your precious baby a dose of reality. You tell her she's a star, tell her she's going to be a big star, but she's not. No one from around here becomes a star of anything. You're just setting her up for heartbreak." Treasure brushed past her and started to storm out of the room, but Gloria grabbed her by the arm.

Treasure, her face aghast at the nerve of someone actually touching her, whirled back toward Gloria.

"I'm serious," Gloria said, her voice low, her jaw tight. "You stay away from my daughter, or I will end you."

Treasure hesitated, as if she couldn't think how to respond to that. But then she tipped her head back and laughed at the high ceiling.

Sandra cringed. Of all the things Treasure could have done or said in that moment, Sandra thought that laugh was probably the most obnoxious and infuriating.

Treasure ripped her arm out of Gloria's grip and left the room still laughing. Sandra hurried to get out of her way.

11

Corina promptly burst into tears, and Gloria took her into her arms, making Sandra suddenly the interloper in the room. She sneaked out, and followed Treasure up the stairs, keeping her distance. Had Otis really upset Treasure that much, that she had to go and take it out on a kid? Or was Treasure just that much of a jerk? And if she was that mean, why did people keep casting her? Did she really sell enough tickets to warrant that? She wasn't *that* beautiful. Along with the disgust Otis had mentioned, Sandra found herself feeling something else for Treasure: pity.

Chapter 4

Sandra was more than relieved to return to her comfy chair and pick up her knitting. She sank back into the cushion and tried not to think about the weather waiting outside. She tried to enjoy watching her son on stage.

They were working on the scene were all the Walton—er, make that Spencer—children were outside having a snowball fight. Even though there were only three of the seven Spencer children present, Frank decided to tweak some blocking. Sandra wasn't looking forward to the chaos that would ensue when the other Spencer children came back to find people standing in their spots. But nor was she about to interfere with Frank's perfectionism. And so, the three kids present ran around the stage screaming and pelting one another with invisible snowballs. It was actually quite amusing, but it was also loud, and the other adults made a big show of being annoyed with the volume and headed downstairs.

Sandra doubted that she would miss them. She was used to loud noises and enjoyed the scene as it evolved in front of her—so much so that she was sad when Frank threw his hands up in the air and said, "Let's move on." He looked around the room and appeared annoyed to see that none of his actors were there. "Corban, let's work on your scene with Grandpa. Would you mind going downstairs to find him?" Frank's voice was spiked with irritation.

"No need! I'm here." Otis materialized near the entrance to the theater.

"Great. Let's go." Frank turned to face the stage as Otis speed-walked to the front of the auditorium and climbed up onto the stage. He sat down in his rocking chair and looked at Frank expectantly. "Go ahead," Frank said.

Otis turned toward Corban and took his hands. Corban looked afraid of him but stood firm. Otis delivered his lines in the most ungrandpalike voice that Sandra had ever heard. Otis's wife had told her that they had children, but she wondered now if they had grandchildren. She doubted it.

Peter sat down in the front row and leaned back in his chair to watch. Sandra quickly lost interest in the scene that did not involve her son and returned to her knitting. But a few minutes later, when she looked up, she saw that cute little Corina had sat down beside Peter and they were head to head, whispering. Part of Sandra was overjoyed at this sight. How adorable! Peter likes a girl! But another part of Sandra was terrified. Peter likes a girl? When did that happen? *How* did that happen? And from the looks of things, she liked him back. She rubbed his arm before getting up and prancing toward the back stairs, leaving Sandra unsure what to think. So, she sat there staring at the back of her son's head, her needles frozen mid-stitch.

She was so intent on staring at her son that Frank startled her when he leaned down to whisper into her ear. "I need to use the facilities. Could you supervise for a minute?"

Her? Supervise a play? Was he mad?

"They won't even know I'm gone." Without waiting for an answer, he patted her on the shoulder and vanished into the shadows behind her.

She turned her attention to the stage and wished she *could* give a few directing points. She would tell Otis to marathon a couple seasons of *The Waltons*. Also, if you're going to play a loving grandpa, you need to pretend that you like your grandson. Poor Corban.

A blood-curdling scream came from the back stairwell. Everyone froze, but Sandra knew it was Corina, and took off running even as her skin broke out in gooseflesh. A lot faster than she used to be only six months ago, she reached the top of the stairs in seconds and found poor Corina staring down at Treasure, who was sprawled out at the bottom of the stairs, one leg cocked off at an unhuman angle. Her eyes were closed, and she was far too still. Sandra grabbed Corina and brought her head to her chest, but it was too late to protect her from the sight. She rubbed the back of her head. "Don't look, honey."

Otis, Corban, and Peter tried to press into the small space to see what was going on, but the small landing could barely accommodate the two people it currently held.

Another, smaller scream sounded from the bottom of the stairs, and the scuffling of many footsteps followed. Gloria came into view with her hand on her cheek. "Is she ... Oh no, is she ..."

"Should we call an ambulance?" someone said.

I don't think that would do much good at this point. "Gloria!" Sandra called down softly.

Gloria looked up, saw her daughter, jumped again, and started to step over Treasure.

"Wait!" Sandra cried. Other faces appeared then and peered up at her expectantly. When had she been put in charge? "Go around! Use the other stairs. If she's ..." She didn't want to finish that sentence and just pointed toward the other end of the building, relieved when Gloria turned to obey. *If she's dead, we should be respectful and not step over her body.*

"It's Treasure," she said to the people behind her. "It looks like she fell down the stairs." She looked at her son and then down at Corina, who was trembling in her arms. "Go with Peter, honey. I need to go help Treasure." Now *there* was something she didn't think she'd ever say. She handed off the shaken child to her son, who was probably a bit shaken himself, and then carefully started down the rickety stairs.

She wanted to believe that Treasure could be helped, but it didn't look that way. The closer she got to her, the more tragic the scene appeared. She had hit the cement floor with her head, which had blood pooled beneath it. Both her legs still rested on the stairs, and Sandra had this urge to straighten them out on the floor for her. She knew she shouldn't touch her, but the poor woman just looked so uncomfortable. She didn't touch her legs, though; instead, she took great care to walk around her, not over her, and then squatted down to feel her neck for a pulse, and she heard someone gasp. What did they want her to do? As she'd anticipated, there was no pulse. "Someone needs to call the police," she said softly.

"There's no signal here!" Otis exclaimed, as if she were stupid.

She wanted to tell him to stop being so rude and obnoxious, but she didn't have the energy. "Billy," she said without looking up. She hadn't seen him, but she assumed he was there. Everyone was there. "Could you please use the theater's phone to call the police?"

"Yes, ma'am." She heard his footsteps on the cement as he walked away.

Starting to stand up, she noticed a hammer under a register, about a foot away from Treasure's partially open hand. What on earth? She looked up the stairs to see Frank staring down at her, apparently paralyzed by what he was seeing. She started up the stairs to check the landing, to see if it was the same hammer that she'd seen there in the pile of tools. As she approached, Frank said, "It was an accident, right?"

Chapter 5

What an interesting thing to say, Sandra thought. She *had* assumed it was an accident. Hadn't everyone? She'd only had second thoughts when she saw the hammer, and no one else—that she knew of, anyway—had seen the hammer. She climbed the last few steps and looked down at the pile of tools. Sure enough: no hammer.

She looked up at Frank. "I don't know if it was an accident. How many times has Treasure been up and down these stairs? This is like a second home to her. Maybe someone pushed her." Frank gasped, and Sandra felt guilty for being so dramatic. But then she looked down at Treasure's lifeless body and didn't feel so guilty anymore. "Maybe it was an accident, but I doubt it."

Frank abruptly grabbed her arm. "Not a word!"

"What?" She yanked her arm out of his grasp.

"Don't say a word about your suspicions. I don't want everyone panicking, and I don't want rumors starting about this theater."

She nodded. "Deal." She would stay as quiet as possible, but not because she was worried about the theater's reputation. If there was a murderer sneaking about, she didn't want to tip her hand. Sandra's eyes surveyed the rest of the landing, looking for other clues. She leaned toward the decrepit handrail for a closer look.

"Stop that," Frank hissed.

A chill went down Sandra's spine. Frank had been in the bathroom when Treasure had fallen, right? So he couldn't have been here, right? So why was he so adamant that she be willfully ignorant about the situation they were in?

He answered the question she hadn't asked aloud: "If you look suspicious, others will catch the suspicion."

"Then go distract them," she said quickly. "I'll just be a minute." She wasn't giving up that spot. There could be clues that someone could easily remove if given a chance.

"Fine." He took a big breath. "Everyone," he called out with a clear, strong voice, "return to the auditorium, please! Use the front stairs."

Frank disappeared, and Sandra resumed her study of the small area. It didn't take long for her to see a narrow, bright red mark on the dingy white wall inside of the handrail. Her stomach turned. That sure looked like Mrs. Walton's shade. She slipped back down the stairs and bent to look at Treasure's right hand, taking care not to touch it. Sure enough, a nail was broken. For the first time, fear made an appearance in Sandra's mind, and she didn't like it. She was going to need some help. She squeezed her eyes shut and silently prayed, "Please, God, send Bob quick." Her eyes popped open as she said amen, and she took another look. Treasure must have grabbed the hammer, right? How else could it have gotten down the stairs and under the register? She could've knocked it off the ledge, but it wasn't likely. The bag of nails was closer to the edge, as was the electric drill, and those things remained unmoved, despite the drill's cord dangling down and begging to be yanked. So, she'd grabbed the hammer, but why? Who breaks their nail on a wall and then reaches for a hammer before plunging backward to her death?

Someone who was pushed—that's who.

Sandra needed Bob. Right now.

While she waited, without confidence that he would ever show up, she continued to examine the landing and the stairs, but didn't see anything else interesting.

"Sandra!"

THE SHOWSTOPPER

She recognized that voice. Jan, the stage manager. The woman was a shrew, an utter control freak, and Sandra was finding it difficult to love her.

"Sandra! Come out here!" she called again.

Giving one last glance around, and hoping Bob was on his way, Sandra stepped back out into the main room to find everyone seated and silent. Corina still cried. Billy looked to be on the verge. She'd known he was a big softie. Peter looked scared, and Sandra quickly went to him, sat down beside him, and put her arm around his shoulders, relieved that he let her.

"We've decided we all need to stay together until the police get here," Jan announced.

Sandra wondered who "we" was. Frank didn't look to be in agreement. In fact, he looked like he was in a colonoscopy waiting room.

"I've gone around the entire perimeter of the building," Billy said softly. "And there are no tire tracks or footprints. So that means one of us is a murderer."

That explained Frank's expression. So much for pretending there'd been an accident.

Jan held up a hand. "Let's not jump to any conclusions. Those stairs are treacherous. I am certain that she simply fell." She glared over her glasses at Billy. "But neither you nor Sandra are police officers, so stop pretending you are." She moved her glare to Sandra. "We will wait here for the police, who will, no doubt, declare that this was an unfortunate accident."

For a moment, everyone was silent, looking around the room to see if anyone was wearing a "murderer" name tag.

"When will they get here?" Peter asked softly.

"Any minute," Jan said, and Sandra laughed out loud.

Worried that her laugh had been a smidgen ill-timed, she hastened to add, "It'll be at least a half-hour."

19

"More than that," Billy said. "It's changed to freezing rain out there."

Chapter 6

Gloria had said, "I will end you" to Treasure just before she died. Sandra had thought she meant that she'd end her career. But had she meant something else? Something more sinister? Surely she hadn't meant that she would literally end Treasure for good? Sandra sneaked a peek at the theater mom who had an arm around each of her children. Tears streamed down her face. Surely a person that sad hadn't murdered someone? Or maybe those were tears of guilt.

Gloria caught Sandra staring at her, and before Sandra could yank her gaze away, Gloria offered her a wan smile. Sandra tried to return the smile, but she feared it looked more like a grimace. As she turned her face front, she caught sight of Bob standing in the corner of the room, near the top of the stairs. Her spirit leapt at the sight of him. Thank the heavens, he was here. She didn't even know why she was so comforted by his presence, but she was. Maybe that's just what happened to people when angels appeared.

He motioned her over. She started to stand up, but then froze. They'd told her to stay here, right? So she wasn't allowed to move? Bob looked confused. She shook her head slightly, unsure how to wordlessly communicate her indecision. But then she decided that she didn't care what they'd told her. "I'll be right back," she whispered to Peter, and then she stood up, trying to look bold and confident.

No one said anything until she took a step toward Bob. Then Jan came to life. "Where do you think you're going?" Her voice was a thousand fingernails on a thousand chalkboards.

Sandra turned her head without turning her body away from her destination. "I'm going to go see if I can figure out what happened."

"No, you're not!" Jan stood up and squared her shoulders. She was ready for a fight. Was this woman going to wrestle her back into her chair?

Sandra almost giggled at the thought. "Yes, I am." She used her even, toneless voice, the same one she used on overly emotional soccer coaches. Out of the corner of her eye, she saw Bob smile.

"We agreed to all stay here and wait for the police!" Jan sounded desperate.

"I didn't agree to anything." She headed for the stairs again.

"It's not safe!" Jan's voice had turned into a roar.

Trying to remain calm, cool, and collected, Sandra turned toward her. "I'll be fine. I'm the only one leaving the room. I'll only be in danger if one of you follows me."

Apparently, that left them all speechless, because no one else said a word. She walked past Bob without acknowledging her invisible friend, and then he followed her through the doorway and onto the landing of the stairs. He gasped when he saw Treasure. "Oh, wow."

"I know," she whispered. "Where was the theater angel?" She was kidding, playing off the fact that Bob was the local middle school sports angel, so shouldn't there be a community theater angel? But the look on Bob's face suggested that her quip was closer to truth than she realized. "What? Is there really a theater angel?"

Bob looked around, as if he expected to see another of his kind lurking about quietly. "Sort of. There's an arts angel. I think this would fall under his purview, but I'm not sure." He looked down at Treasure and shook his head.

"Can you help?" Sandra was sure that he could. She didn't even know why she'd asked.

At first he didn't answer, and she got a little worried he was going to ditch her. "I can try." He looked at her and smiled. "I'll try."

"Thank you."

"So, what do you know so far?"

"Not much. Treasure had no qualms about having enemies. Just tonight she had an argument with Otis, was horribly mean to Matthew, though he probably deserved it, and was a total bully to Corina. I know Corina didn't throw her down the stairs, because she was upstairs when Treasure fell." Right? Wasn't she? Just *when had* Treasure fallen? "I think. Anyway, and Corina's mum witnessed the bullying and was justifiably enraged."

"How enraged?"

"She was pretty mad. She threatened her—"

Peter appeared in the doorway. "Mom?" His face was pale as a sheet. "Who are you talking to?"

"No one!" she snapped. "Go back to your seat!" She sounded far harsher than she'd wanted to, but she really didn't want her son to think she was talking to herself. Looking injured, he turned and trudged away from her. She would have to apologize mightily for that one. She returned her attention to the angel.

"You haven't told him about me?"

She shook her head. "I thought you didn't want me to!"

"I didn't, but I still figured you told your family."

Should she tell him now that she'd told her husband? Nah, not necessary, especially since he hadn't even considered believing her. "Well, you shouldn't make assumptions."

Seeming pleased with her silence, Bob looked down at Treasure. "So, how do we know she didn't just fall?"

"Because ..." She pointed to the empty spot on the ledge. "Before she fell, there was a hammer lying right there." Then she pointed to the ancient register along the wall by Treasure's outstretched arm. "And now the hammer is down there."

"So you think someone hit her with a hammer?" Bob sounded overly alarmed. "Has anyone called the police?"

"Yes, Billy called them ..." As she spoke the words, she wondered if they were true. How did she *know* he'd called them? Just because she liked him didn't mean he wasn't a murderer. Maybe he had only pretended to call the police and now he was going to pick them off one by one. A shiver passed down her spine as she shook her head. "I think they've been called, maybe we should double check that, and no, I don't think anyone hit her with a hammer."

"Why not?"

"Because I don't see any hammer imprints on her"—she knew such a mark could easily be on the back of her head, but she didn't vocalize that—"and because I think she was using the hammer to defend herself."

Bob looked confused. "That didn't go well."

"No. But look." She pointed toward the shiny red smear on the wall. "I think this came from her fingernail. I think she was trying to grab for the banister, to stop herself from falling, but there's no way her finger could have gotten in there to leave that smudge if she were holding a hammer."

Bob still looked confused. Maybe he wasn't going to be much help after all.

She took a deep breath and pretended she was explaining something to her seven-year-old. "So she must have picked up the hammer afterward. I think she almost fell once, grabbed the handrail to stop herself, broke her nail, and then grabbed the hammer to defend herself, and then fell for real." Suddenly, she was overcome with doubt. Who was she to be so confident in throwing out theories like that? "I think. Maybe."

Bob either didn't notice her wave of doubt or ignored it. He was staring at the register. "Is there anything on the hammer?"

"Uh ... I didn't check. I thought it best not to touch anything."

Bob vanished from his spot. If she'd gotten used to this trick back in September, she had forgotten. It startled her now and left her feeling uneasy. He reappeared at the bottom of the stairs, looking up at her. "I don't see anything on the hammer."

Sandra was surprised that he could see something that was tucked up against a wall under a register. She was not surprised that there was nothing on the hammer.

Bob glanced down at Treasure. "She doesn't have anything in her pockets either."

"I didn't realize you had X-ray vision."

"I don't always. It's hard to explain."

Sandra felt she was missing something. But what? She crept down the stairs, trying to be hyperaware of her surroundings, trying to see everything with fresh eyes. There was something else—she just knew it. She stepped over poor Treasure's leg and then knelt beside her left hand, the one that hadn't held the hammer. But hadn't she seen her holding something in that hand? Something shiny—

"Her phone!" Sandra cried, too loudly, popping up like a fully cranked jack-in-the-box. She looked at Bob. "Where's her phone?"

Bob didn't answer.

"Are you *sure* her pockets are empty?"

He nodded.

"Then her phone is missing. I've *never* seen her without it, even though we have no signal here. She carries it around with her like it's attached to her skin. She even has it on stage. Drives the director nuts—

"Mom?" The timid voice came from the top of the stairs.

Sandra looked up.

"You're scaring me."

Chapter 7

Bummer. Scaring her son was the last thing Sandra wanted to do. "Honey? Can you come down here, please? I'll explain. Go use the front stairs."

Peter hesitated. "I don't know if they'll let me."

"You're right. Hang on." She grudgingly stepped back over Treasure's leg, again tempted to move it to a more seemly position, and then scooted up the stairs to her son. "Let's go together." She resisted the urge to take his hand into her own, but then, as if he'd read her mind, he slid his fingers into her palm, and she squeezed them as they headed up the sloped center aisle of the auditorium. It appeared no one else had moved. Everyone stared as they passed.

"Now where are you going?" Jan screeched, and Sandra flinched at the pitch of that caterwaul.

She didn't answer the overbearing stage manager, and pulled Peter along a little faster behind her. But just before she started down the stairs, she had a second thought, and pulled Peter into the ticket office, where the phone was. She tried to be silent as she pulled the door shut behind her, but it clicked loudly into place. Fearing they'd soon be interrupted, she hurried to dial 911.

"Who are you calling?" Peter whispered.

"Cops." She wished she had her purse with her so she could locate Detective Chip Buker's direct number.

"Billy already called them."

"Shh—"

The ringing stopped. "911. Do you require police, fire, or ambulance?"

She hesitated, wondering just how ridiculous she was being, and then identified herself, gave her location, and asked if police were en route.

"Ma'am, this line is for emergencies—"

"I know, and this *is* an emergency. Are the police on their way?"

"Yes, ma'am, they are. Please be patient—"

"Thank you," Sandra said, without letting her finish. She hung up the phone. Good. Billy was a good guy. Her judge of character wasn't great, but at least it wasn't abysmal. She took Peter's hand again and together they sneaked out of the room and down the stairs into the basement. Nearly every room in the building was on this bottom level, as most of the first floor was taken up by the auditorium itself.

As Peter descended behind her, he whispered, "What is going on, Mom?"

She got to the basement and looked around for Bob. She didn't see him. She turned toward her son and took him by the shoulders. "Honey, I need you to trust me right now."

He nodded.

She wasn't convinced. "I mean *really* trust me, even if part of you doesn't want to. I need you to trust me."

He nodded with more vigor. "Yes, Mum, of course I trust you!" His face looked too pale in the dim light.

"Okay, good. As you may have guessed, Treasure was definitely murdered. There is evidence. So I think you should stay with me until the police get here. I'm sorry that I left you. But I had a good reason." She took a deep breath. "I'm sorry, but I've been keeping a secret from you. The truth is ..." She took a gulp of air. "The truth is that I've been talking to an angel. An honest to God, supernatural angel. He helped me get out of that little scrape with you-know-who back in September, and I've asked him to come here now to—"

Peter interrupted her with a bold laugh that sounded eerily like his father. It was a good thing she loved his father.

"I know. I had a hard time believing it too, when Bob first appeared to me."

Peter laughed even harder. A tear leaked out of the corner of his right eye. He gasped for air. "The angel's name is Bob?"

She put a hand on his shoulder. "Yes, and, honey, we're in a tight spot right now, so I need you to focus. We can laugh and talk about this later. But for now, know that if I'm talking to someone, it's him. I don't know if he'll allow you to see him."

Peter stopped laughing. "He's invisible?"

Why was this such a surprise? "Yes. Usually. He lets me see him, and Sammy can see him." Just saying her baby's name made her miss him, but she was grateful he was home safe with Dad. They were both blissfully unaware that she'd somehow gotten tangled up in another murder scene.

"Come on, he's probably still with Treasure." She took Peter's hand and led him across the large basement until she saw Bob standing right where she'd left him, scowling at her. "Bob, you know my son Peter. I've told him everything."

Bob nodded as if he'd expected that. "I wish you hadn't done that."

"I had to. I didn't want my son thinking I was nuts."

Bob stared at Peter for several seconds and then looked at Sandra. "I'm here as a favor to you, remember?"

She didn't see how this connected to her telling Peter the truth. "I know, and I'm grateful."

Bob ran a hand through his short curly hair and looked at Peter again. "Okay, but, Peter, please don't tell anyone else about me. I'm not supposed to be flitting around the county appearing to people."

Sandra looked at Peter to see if he'd heard Bob's voice, and his eyes were wide as saucers. She took his hand. "Are you okay, honey?"

He nodded once, slowly. "I see him."

Good. So that was out of the way. "I'm glad. Thank you, Bob, for letting him see you. That makes my life much easier. But, Peter, you really can't tell anyone about him, okay? It's serious."

Peter nodded, his brow knitted. "Is your name really Bob?"

Sandra gasped, a little embarrassed at his impertinence. She tried to remind herself that she was asking him to process a lot right now. Someone he knew had probably been murdered; there was probably a murderer in their midst; and he'd just met a supernatural being. A supernatural being whose name just happened to be Bob.

To her relief, Bob chuckled. "Sort of. My name is Binadab. It means, 'My father is generous.' But for the last few centuries, it's just been simpler to call myself Bob."

This information threw Sandra for a loop. Was he suggesting people nowadays were too stupid to pronounce his name? Should she be offended? Could *she* pronounce his name? She tried. And failed. "Is that Hebrew?"

He nodded. "Don't worry about the pronunciation. It's kind of you to try, but I meant it when I said Bob was easier. For everyone. And I really don't mind Bob. It seems to suit me."

It did suit him. This was true. But his Hebrew name seemed to suit him too.

Chapter 8

"I've looked everywhere," Bob said. "I even went upstairs and looked in what I assume was Treasure's purse. But I didn't find any phone."

How mysterious. Sandra thought for a second. "Can you use your X-ray vision to look in other people's pockets, see if the phone's there?"

He shook his head rapidly. "No way."

She gave him a second to expound. He didn't. "Does that mean you're not allowed to or you are unable to?"

He gave her a frazzled look, as if he was tired of dealing with mere humans. "I don't know if I am able to, but I won't."

An angel who cared about civil liberties. How kind. "I guess *I* could go frisk them all?"

This made Peter look nervous. "No, Mom, don't."

But Bob appeared to be thinking that option over. "Nah, I doubt the murderer still has it in his pocket. I bet he hid it somewhere. Or threw it out a window. That's what I'd do."

"What makes you so sure the murderer is a *he*? Gloria was really mad at Treasure. She had good reason to be furious—"

"Mom, Mrs. Trembley would never hurt someone."

Just because you like her daughter doesn't make the woman innocent. "I think you're right, but I would have said that of everyone here."

Peter shook his head. "I definitely think Jan could kill someone. She is *mean*."

She couldn't argue with that, so she turned to Bob. "If we can't go search people, then what's our next step?"

He rubbed his chin, making Sandra wonder if angels had to shave. And even if they did, did *this* one have to? He had such a baby face. "I wish I knew."

The lights flickered and then went out, plunging them into a complete darkness that was eerily silent.

"Got a flashlight?" Bob asked.

"No, and my phone's in the car." She never brought it into the theater. Why would she, when they were in a complete dead zone? She vowed to never leave it in the car again. "Can't you just make some supernatural light? Turn on your halo or something?"

"I could," Bob said, his voice tinged with irritation, "but we don't know who is where, and we don't want someone seeing an ethereal glow, now do we?"

"We know where everyone is. They're all sitting upstairs," Sandra said.

"Not anymore. Several people are moving about. Some are heading down the front stairs already."

Sandra strained to listen, but couldn't hear anything. "I can't hear anything," she whispered.

"You don't have angel ears."

Peter snickered beside her.

"Okay, I don't want to stand here in the dark beside a dead body. Can we go upstairs? I'm already cold."

"The temperature hasn't changed yet," Bob whispered. "That's in your head."

It was Sandra's turn to be annoyed with Bob, but she didn't want to argue with him. "I'm going upstairs." She felt around for Peter's hand, grabbed it, and started pulling him back the way they'd come. Now she *could* hear rustling. Footsteps, several of them, and a cabinet door banged shut. There was a crash, and someone—Otis, she thought—said a naughty word. So much for keeping all the suspects safely contained. She stopped walking and put a hand out in front of her to feel for the stairwell.

"We're not there yet, Mom." Peter pulled her ahead with alarming speed.

She saw a flash of light in the kitchen area. Someone had brought their phone in. Or maybe they were using Treasure's phone. "Wait." She started to pull Peter toward the kitchen.

"No, Mom! I want to go upstairs." He was scared. She couldn't stand the sound of that, so she let him start pulling again. Soon, he said, "Here, I found the railing."

She reached out and groped in the darkness until she too found the banister. The feel of it beneath her hand made her think of Treasure's panicked attempt to grab her handrail, and Sandra shuddered in the darkness. Peter had already started up the stairs. She stuck her foot out and hit the bottom step with her toe. Then, with painful slowness, she started her ascent. She heard someone coming down toward them and clutched Peter's hand even tighter, pulling him toward their right. The mystery person passed without word or incident. Sandra really didn't like not being able to tell who it was. She wanted to keep a bead on each and every person in the theater.

As they arrived on the first floor, small lights flitting around in the auditorium cast a pale light into the foyer. Sandra would take it. She could see the floor in front of her, at least. Peter picked up speed as he pulled her toward the light, which turned out to be three cell phones. She squinted, trying to make out who she was looking at. Ethel gave her a little wave, and she pulled Peter that way. She sat down beside her and let out a long breath.

"Take a load off." Ethel giggled, again surprising Sandra with her good mood.

"Where is everybody going?" Sandra looked around, trying to figure out who was missing, and wondering where Bob had gone.

"Went to look for candles. Some people didn't have their phones."

A thought occurred to Sandra, and she wanted to kick herself for not thinking about it before. "Ethel, do you want to sneak out?"

Ethel laughed. "Aren't we supposed to stick around until the police get here?"

Sandra leaned closer to her. "Yes, but I know you're not the murderer, and I know Peter isn't. I don't see the harm in you two trying to make a break—"

"I wouldn't try it," Billy said from behind her, and she jumped. Hadn't she been whispering? She turned to look at him. "I just went outside to see about the power," he explained, "and it is glare ice out there."

"See about the power?" Sandra repeated. "Didn't the storm knock it out?"

"It seems so, yes, but I wasn't so sure at first."

"You mean, you thought the killer cut the power?" Why hadn't she thought of that? She was a terrible sleuth.

Chapter 9

"Maybe I should just stay put," Ethel said, and Sandra grudgingly agreed.

She didn't want to drive on the ice either. "I guess neither option, going or staying, is very safe." She looked at her son, overwhelmed by the desire to protect him. Where was Bob?

A scream sounded from directly beneath her, and her blood ran cold. She jumped up and headed for the door, along with nearly everyone else in the room, but then she stopped and turned back toward Ethel. "Would you mind watching Peter for a sec—"

"I don't need to be watched, Mom. I'm not a baby."

"You're right, honey. I'm sorry. But would you stay here with Ethel? I'll be right back." But then, as the last person left the room, taking the last cell with them, they were plunged into darkness again. "Never mind," she said, sitting back down. Her skin was itching in protest. She needed to go see what the screaming was about, but she couldn't leave these two in the darkness.

Ethel sensed her unease. "Sorry, I'd go with you, but I don't think I should be stumbling about in the darkness at my age."

"I know. And I wouldn't want you to. I just really want to know what's going on."

They sat in the silent darkness for what felt like forever, until a small flame bobbed into view, throwing a pleasant circle of light around the room. Sandra quickly scanned the room before turning to identify the light-bearer.

It was Gloria. "I found some candles." She carried a plastic shopping bag full of candles of every size, color, and level of consumption.

"What was that scream?" Sandra asked.

"Sorry if it scared you. Sound sure does carry with the furnace off. It was just Corina. The cat jumped out from behind something and scared her half to death."

The explanation left Sandra both relieved and disappointed. Not that she'd hoped for another dead body, but an attempted assault with a few witnesses would help solve the puzzle.

"Cat? What cat?" Ethel sounded alarmed.

"It's Frank's cat," Sandra explained, as Gloria used the lighted candle to light the candle in her other hand. "They have a severe mice problem here, so he brings his cat in to scare them off. Her name is Hildegarde."

Gloria handed the newly lit candle to Ethel, who was laughing so hard the flame shook in her hand. "Hildegarde? Who names a cat Hildegarde?"

"Frank Flamatti, that's who. He's got another one at home named Leopold. Sorry, I haven't found any candle stands yet. I'm still looking, but at least you'll be able to see." She pulled a third candle out of the bag and handed it to Sandra before lighting it.

"Thank you." Sandra was grateful for the stubby stick of wax in her hand.

"Don't mention it. I'll be back. I'm just going to go see if anyone downstairs needs one. And I'll look for more."

"If you see any blankets, grab those too, would you?" Ethel asked.

"Absolutely." Gloria turned to go.

Sandra had to fight not to follow her.

"Go ahead," Ethel said. "I know you're dying to."

Sandra flew out of her seat. "I don't need to go now that we know who screamed and why, but I will go get you a blanket." Sandra fled before Ethel could change her mind. She moved so fast that her candle almost went out, and she forced herself to slow down. "Bob, where are you and your superpower hearing, anyway?" she muttered under her breath.

There was no response.

She found her way to the props room without seeing anyone. At first, she thought the door was locked, and vowed to learn how to pick a lock, but then she realized the old door was just stuck shut, and she lowered her shoulder to give it some more encouragement. It opened, and the smell of mothballs washed over her. Would Ethel rather have mothball blankets or be cold? She really didn't know, but she thought she'd leave it up to Ethel. She entered the stinky room and closed the door behind her—not because she desired privacy, but because she didn't want anyone sneaking up on her.

She'd thought finding a blanket in a prop room would be a simple task, but it wasn't. She'd never seen such a random collection of artifacts. There were enough holiday decorations to outfit the Disney Christmas Parade. She hadn't realized there were that many plastic holly berries in the world. She pushed her way through the holiday cheer and abruptly found herself in the Halloween section. This was no better. She hurried through the stacks of cobwebs and witch hats and then found herself weaving through supplies from a nineteenth century one-room school house. She stopped in the middle of the room and looked around. *Were* there any blankets? A rustling to her right caused her to whirl around, a movement that somehow made the giant chalkboard to her left come crashing to the ground. Luckily, it hit a pile of old hymnals before it hit the floor, so it didn't shatter, but it still made quite a ruckus. She held her breath, trying to hear if anyone was nearby, unsure why she was so worried about getting caught in the prop room. No, of course, she wouldn't be snooping around in here under normal circumstances. But these weren't normal circumstances.

THE SHOWSTOPPER

Suddenly, she was scared to death for Peter. She shouldn't have left him. Sure, Ethel would try to protect him, but what could she do? She hurried back toward the door, and was almost there when she spotted a box among the Christmas chaos. It was marked "Bedding." Based on the organization of the room, Sandra wasn't confident the box actually *contained* bedding, but it was worth a shot. She navigated her way through the piles of old luggage, telephones, and plastic fruit until she reached the box. She opened it, bracing herself for more foul odors, but there were none, and sure enough, the blanket box contained blankets. She ripped the top two out of the box and then hurried for the door, moving as fast as her little flame would let her.

By now, she was closer to the back stairs than the front, so she headed that way, even though that would mean skirting poor Treasure's body. Where on earth were the police? They should be there by now! She found Bob right where she'd left him, standing beside Treasure, looking down at her face.

"What are you doing?" she whispered.

"Waiting for someone to tamper with the evidence."

Sandra looked around. "And no one has?"

"No, not yet. Everyone is avoiding this area of the building. I think most of them are in the green room."

"Okay, good. I've got to go check on Peter. I left him upstairs."

"You *left* him?"

"Only for two seconds. I just came down to get blankets." But in reality, she didn't know how long she'd been gone. Just how many seconds had she spent exploring the prop room? She took the stairs two at a time, grateful for her new soccer official legs. Soccer season had ended in November, but since then she'd been reffing for an indoor women's league, and those women were *fast*. Sandra was in the best shape of her life. She reached the top of the stairs, and her heart fell toward her feet. Why was the auditorium so dark?

37

Maybe the light from my candle is overpowering Ethel's. Maybe hers is still lit, but I just can't see it. Hoping this wasn't wishful thinking, she walked deeper into the auditorium to see that Ethel and Peter were gone.

Chapter 10

"Peter!" Sandra cried out into the quiet. *God, please let him be all right. I'm sorry that I left them alone.* She hurried toward their seats and found that Ethel hadn't in fact disappeared. She was just tipped over in her seat. A sickness washed over Sandra. Had this stupid play gotten Ethel killed? If so, Sandra knew she could never live with herself. Why had she left them? That had been so stupid! With a trembling hand, she reached out for Ethel's neck, which, praise be, was quite warm. And there was a pulse. Oh thank the heavens. She shook her gently. "Ethel?" She looked her over and didn't see any obvious wounds or blood. What had happened? "Ethel?"

No response. She covered her up with the thickest blanket and then headed back to the office for the phone. They now needed an ambulance as well as the police. And she had to report a kidnapping.

She dialed the number. Was she sure Peter had been kidnapped? No, of course she couldn't be entirely sure, but he wouldn't have just left Ethel there. Something was wrong. It took her several silent seconds to realize the phone wasn't working. She hung up and tried again. No dial tone. She hadn't noticed that the first time. Did that mean that the storm had knocked the phone line out? Or had it been cut?

She was far more scared than she had been during her own kidnapping ordeal. Then, she'd just been *mad* and totally focused on finding a way out. But *now*, this was her *kid*. Her precious Peter. If anything happened to him, she didn't even want to think about what she'd do to the person responsible. She squeezed her eyes shut and prayed fervently. *Please, Father, let this be nothing. Let Peter have wandered off. Send him back right now. And if he was taken somewhere, please protect him. Send your angels—*

She needed to tell Bob.

She headed back through the auditorium to go down the back steps, and she saw Ethel stir. She hurried to her side. "Ethel? Are you okay?"

Her eyelids fluttered open, and she looked around, obviously confused. "I like mashed potatoes."

Oh dear. "I do too, Ethel. Do you remember what happened?"

She looked around the dark room. "To the potatoes?"

"No. To you. Just a few minutes ago."

Some part of her brain came to. "Oh! I was here with Peter." She looked around wildly. "Where's Peter?"

"I don't know. What happened?"

"We were just sitting here, and then something hit me, I think. Where's Peter?"

Poor Ethel. Sandra vowed to never recruit anyone into acting again. "Peter's not here. Her eyes got hot and wet, and she scooched down to search the sloped floor for Ethel's candle. Of course, she couldn't find it.

"Where's Judah?"

The kingdom? Or was that a person? "I'm sorry, what?"

"My son, Judah. I shouldn't have left him alone." Ethel reached up to touch the back of her head and winced. "I've got quite an egg, in fact."

All of Ethel's children were grown up and on their own. "I'm so sorry, Ethel. I didn't mean to put you in danger, but I'm sure Judah is fine."

Ethel guffawed. "It's not your fault, darlin'. You didn't cast a psychopath in *The Waltons*."

"I'm not so sure it was a cast member," Sandra muttered. "I need to go look for Peter, but I don't want to leave you here. Can you walk?"

With both hands, she clasped the seat in front of her and pulled. "I reckon so," she said, coming up to a crooked, wobbly stand. "Let's go. Before the potatoes get cold."

Unsure whether she should move Ethel or not, but thinking it was probably better than leaving her alone, Sandra hooked her hand around Ethel's elbow and forced herself to be patient as they headed for the front stairs.

They went down them with painful slowness, as Sandra fought back tears. She wanted to cry out to Bob, but she didn't want to have to explain that to Ethel.

They finally made it to the basement. "Peter!" Sandra called out.

Otis appeared in front of her, startling her. "What's wrong?" He actually sounded concerned. Maybe terrible situations brought out the best in Otis.

"Someone took Peter." She moved to walk past him, and he let her pass. "Peter!" she called down the hallway.

"Took him?" Otis repeated. "Why do you think someone took him?"

She didn't have time for this. "Because he isn't where I left him."

Otis turned and followed her down the hallway. "But couldn't he have just wandered off? Maybe he went to look for a flashlight. That's what most people are doing."

"No. I told him to stay put. He wouldn't have left without telling me." She wasn't sure why she was leaving a certain detail out of her story, namely that someone had bonked poor Ethel on the noggin.

"Okay, I'll help you look."

She turned to look at him. "You will?" He held his phone's light pointed at the floor, and the weird light it cast on his face made him look older. Her eyes traveled up and down his frame. Suddenly, he looked more fragile than he had looked to her in the past. More harmless. He wasn't an ogre. He was just a grumpy old man. "Thank you," she managed. "I appreciate that."

"You're welcome. Where have you looked?"

"He's not in the auditorium or the office. And then I came here." She wondered if she was making sense.

"Okay, I'll go look in the kitchen." But he made no move to head toward the kitchen. He just stood where he was.

Billy appeared out of the shadows. "What are we looking for?" Billy held a candle out in front of him. He'd managed to find an ancient candlestick. She reckoned that at some point, Mountain View's holiday play had been *The Christmas Carol*.

"Peter," Sandra said. "He's missing."

"You're kidding." Billy's face fell so dramatically that Peter could have been his own kid. "Have you looked outside?"

Sandra shook her head.

"I'll help you look."

"You take the kitchen," Otis hurried to say. "You've already ventured outside enough tonight."

Billy nodded. "Okay. Holler if you need extra help out there. There's a lot of ground to cover." He reached out and gave Sandra's shoulder a gentle squeeze. "We'll find him." He looked at Otis. "In fact, we should probably both go look outside. But I'll check the kitchen first."

Otis didn't look pleased at this decision, and Sandra suspected Otis didn't like Billy much.

She blinked back tears. She didn't trust her voice enough to thank the men, so she just turned and headed toward the spot where Treasure lay.

"Don't tell anyone I said this, but I don't like him very much," Ethel said from behind her.

Sandra slowed to let her catch up to the candlelight she held. "Who, Billy?"

"No," Ethel said quickly. "That Otis feller."

Sandra was tempted to agree with her, but Otis had just shown her a lot of kindness, so she stayed mute.

"Not that I'm calling him a murderer or anything. I just don't like him." She paused, and then, she muttered to herself, "I think he ate my potatoes."

Up ahead, Sandra made out the outline of two people standing near the back stairs. As she got closer, she saw it was only one person—and one angel.

Chapter 11

Matthew stood staring down at the woman he had so admired, and Bob stood staring at Matthew. The scene was a little creepy. Couldn't Matthew feel Bob's eyes on him? Apparently not.

As they approached, Matthew looked up at them, self-consciously wiping his eyes. "Sorry." He sniffed. "I just can't believe she's gone."

"I'm so sorry for your loss." She was sorry, but more than that, she was eager to share some information with Bob, without appearing to be talking to her imaginary friend. So she pretended to talk to Matthew. "Have you seen Peter? Someone took him. Someone knocked Ethel out with a blow to the head and then took my son somewhere." Her voice cracked and she fought to breathe through her panic.

Bob's eyes were wide with concern.

Matthew's were not. Either he hadn't heard her, or he didn't care.

Bob motioned toward the top of the stairs.

"I'd like to go back upstairs," she said slowly, still pretending to talk to Matthew, "but I can't leave Ethel." She didn't dare look at Ethel as she waited for Bob to figure out what she was saying.

"The props room then," Bob said aloud.

Sandra nodded and then looked at Ethel. "Let's go look in the props room."

Ethel, seeming to know that there was more going on than she was aware of, nodded her assent. "Where's the props room?"

"I'll show you." On their way there, Sandra almost smashed into Otis, who was coming out of the costume room.

"Just putting on some extra layers, so I don't freeze to death outside," he said, answering a question no one had asked.

THE SHOWSTOPPER

Sandra didn't care what Otis was doing in the costume room. To each his own. She was in a hurry to get into the props room, and once again, had to lower her shoulder to get the door open. Bob was already inside. He couldn't have opened the door for her? She took a deep breath and tried to think. How could she say what she needed to say to Bob while pretending to talk to Ethel? She looked into Ethel's eyes and slowly said, "I'm scared to death. I need some supernatural help here. I need to find my son."

She'd never seen Ethel's eyes so somber. Ethel reached out and took her hands. Then she began to pray in a voice so strong it gave Sandra the shivers. "Father in heaven, I sense that you have already sent your angels to minister to us in this fearful situation. I ask you for a miracle, knowing full well that you are capable. You have promised to keep your sheep safe, and that's what we need right now, God. Bring this child back to us, using whatever means necessary—"

"Ethel," Bob interrupted, and Ethel's eyes sprang open. "I am an angel of the Lord, and I'm going to help you find Peter."

Whether it was the head injury or Ethel just expected the supernatural, she hardly seemed surprised. "Amen," she said with reverence. She squeezed Sandra's hands. Then she looked at Bob. "Do you have the potatoes?"

Bob looked at Sandra. "You keep looking here. I'm going to go get a bird's eye view."

"Thank you," Sandra said, but her voice came out hoarse.

Bob glanced at Sandra's candle, which had shrunk significantly. "First, let me get you a flashlight." He vanished then, and Sandra opened her mouth to ask Ethel what she thought of Bob, but he reappeared before she could get a word out, and handed Ethel a flashlight that was about three feet long. It was big enough to be a weapon. Maybe that would be a good thing.

Bob vanished again, and Sandra looked around the now well-lit prop room.

With Ethel's new beacon lighting the place up, the room seemed much smaller. "I'm pretty sure Peter's not in here," Ethel said. "Let's go check the costume room."

"Otis just came out of there. I think he would have said something if Peter was in there."

"Let's go check anyway." Ethel turned and headed for the door.

"I was much more alarmed than you when I first saw Bob," Sandra said, and they stepped out into the hallway.

"Bob's not my first angel encounter."

Really? Sandra wanted to ask her for details, but they heard commotion in the green room area, so they headed that way to find Jan trying to herd everyone back into the auditorium.

"Why can't we just stay here?" Gloria asked. "As long as we're all in the same place, isn't that the point?"

Jan looked stymied.

Sandra expected she didn't even have a reason to get them all back to the auditorium, except that this was where she'd initially told them to stay put, and she expected to be obeyed.

"It's warmer down here," Gloria added.

Sandra doubted this. The theater was cooling off rapidly, and that went for every room she'd been in.

"Everyone needs to go back upstairs—" Jan said again, but Sandra interrupted her.

"Actually, I need people to spread out."

Jan opened her mouth, but Sandra didn't let her object.

"Someone has taken my son, and I need help looking for him."

"No one would *take* your son," Jan said in a patronizing tone that made Sandra want to throttle her. "People always think their children are angels, and they never are. If your son is missing, that's because he wandered off on his own. These people need to stay together for their own safety, not run off on some fool's errand chasing your fool son—"

THE SHOWSTOPPER

Ethel stepped right in front of Jan and peered up into her face. "With all due respect, you need to shut your trap." She looked past Jan's shoulder at the others clustered in the room. "I was upstairs with Peter, and someone hit me in the back of the head hard enough to knock me out." Then she looked at Jan again. "So the only fool here is you." She stepped back. "Please, help us look for the child. There is a murderer in our midst, so you should probably go out in twos."

Chapter 12

Peter wasn't in the costume room, though it took a minute to determine this for sure. Much like the prop room, the costume room was a disaster. Sandra had never seen so many stovepipe hats in one place. Had they hosted an Abraham Lincoln impersonator contest? It also appeared that every child dancer within a hundred miles had donated every costume they'd ever worn. And Sandra didn't even want to touch the pile of animal costumes in the back corner. She continued to hope that they were, in fact, only costumes.

"At least this room doesn't smell like mothballs," Ethel said.

"No, it doesn't. It smells kind of good. What is that smell?"

"No idea. Smells like a truck stop bathroom."

Sandra didn't wholly agree with this assessment, but the association made her no longer appreciate the scent.

"Let's get out of here." Ethel shuffled toward the door.

"Wait. It's only going to get colder. Let's put on some more layers." She poked through the racks like she was in a thrift-store-shopping-race and came out with a shawl for Ethel, a flannel and an oversized coat for herself, and a sweatshirt and coat for Peter. "Okay, now let's go."

Over the next twenty minutes, Ethel became Sandra's favorite person. Though she moved slowly and uttered the occasional mention of potatoes or whimper of pain, she led the charge as the two of them searched every nook and cranny of the theater, all the while saying encouraging, soothing things like: "Don't worry. We'll find him. He'll be fine."

They were just about to duck into the sound room when Bob reappeared. "I found him."

Sandra let out a cry of relief and flung her arms around Bob's neck. "Where is he?"

"Come on, I'll take you to him."

"You left him?"

Bob held a finger to his lips, and then turned and walked to the front of the building. Sandra hurried to follow, and Ethel fell behind. When they got to the front door of the theater, Bob stopped to wait.

"She'll catch up, Bob! Let's go! Where is he?"

"He's fine. I locked him in, so no one can get to him."

"Locked him in where?" she cried.

Bob stayed frustratingly silent until Ethel joined them. Then he said to her, "Peter's outside, but it's mighty cold and slippery out there. I can lock you into the office if you want. You don't have to go with us—"

"I'm going." Ethel stuck her chin out. "I love that child. You'll just have to use your supernatural powers to keep me on my feet."

Despite the panic tightening Sandra's chest, she had to smile at that.

"Very well." Bob opened the front door, and the wind stole Sandra's breath away. She wrapped her arms around her chest and followed Bob down the front steps and across what would be the front lawn in the spring.

"From above, it was easy to see the trail they left," Bob said, and it was hard to hear his voice as the wind tried to carry it away. "The snow and ice are already obscuring their tracks, but it was clear that Peter put up a good fight the whole way to the shed."

"The shed?" Sandra exclaimed, and as the cold rushed in, was soon sorry she'd tried to exclaim anything. She clamped her mouth shut and put her head down. What shed? She hadn't known the theater had a shed.

"Yes, the shed. It's got gardening supplies in it. And a lawn mower. We're almost there."

Sandra took his word for it. She couldn't see anything but white.

A few steps later, Bob stopped. Sandra pulled up before running into him and squinted through the icy mix falling from the sky. Sure enough, there was a shed there. Bob reached out and opened the door, without touching any lock, leaving Sandra to believe the lock had been of the supernatural variety. She pushed past Bob to step inside, where she found a smiling Peter. She wrapped him in a bear hug. "What are you smiling about?" She was almost mad at him for being happy.

"Because Bob already found me," he mumbled into her shoulder.

She felt the others pushing in behind her, and then the door shut, instantly warming the inside of the unheated shed. She hurriedly forced Peter into the sweatshirt, which was at least five sizes too big, and then tried to get him to put the coat on. He refused, so she told him to hold it.

"Are you okay?" Peter asked Ethel.

"I'm feeling a bit loopy, but I'll live."

No one had any flashlights or candles, yet Sandra could see. She traced the source of the light to Bob's hands, which were glowing softly. Neat trick. "Why did you leave him here?" Sandra said, her voice laden with accusation.

Bob held up one glowing hand to ward off her verbal attack. "Let's think about this. Why would someone grab Peter and stuff him, unharmed, into a shed?"

Peter started to say something, but Bob shushed him. "Hang on. Really, I think it's important we know why."

"Wasn't Peter about to tell you why?" Sandra asked.

Bob shook his head. "No, Peter was about to say something else."

"How do you know?" Ethel cried. "Can you read minds?"

"Certainly not. But after a few millennia of dealing with humans, I am fairly intuitive. Now *think*."

Sandra thought. "I have no idea. Why don't you just tell us your theory, Matlock?"

"I think that the murderer did it."

What a shocking theory. We never would have thought of that.

"And I think the fact that Peter remains unharmed tells us a lot about this murderer."

"Like what? He or she likes kids?"

"Definitely a he," Peter said. "Or a woman who smells manly and has a hairy arm."

Oddly, Sandra thought of Esau, but then decided he probably wasn't in on this. And she suddenly had a craving for a hot bowl of stew.

"No," Bob said. "I mean, maybe. Lots of people like kids. But I think this shows that the murderer isn't prone to violence. It's not his first choice. I think Treasure's death was an accident. I'm not saying she fell alone, but I don't think whoever killed her meant to kill her."

"Okay," Sandra said, failing to understand why he found this line of reasoning important. "I guess that's a source of comfort?"

"Exactly. But it's more than that. The person stuffed *Peter* in the shed," Bob said. "He hasn't touched anyone else—"

"I beg to differ," Ethel announced. "He certainly touched me."

"Okay, sorry, he hit you, but he didn't *take* you. Yet, he took Peter, which leads me to wonder why."

"Why?" Sandra cried. "Get to the point, Bob!"

"I think he took Peter to distract *you*, Sandra. *You* specifically. So, why would he do that? Because you're onto him. He figured if you were busy looking for your son, you wouldn't be trying to figure out who killed Treasure—"

"Or, he took the weakest person he could take, in order to distract everyone," Peter said.

Bob shook his head. "I don't think so. I saw by the tracks in the snow that you put up quite a fight," Bob said, and Peter beamed with pride. "It would have been easier to take Corina or Corban, or even Ethel. Yet, he took you." Bob looked at Sandra. "Which makes me think that he fears Sandra finding him out."

"But I don't have a clue!" Sandra cried.

Bob nodded again. "I know that. But I don't think the murderer knows that. So, how can we use that to our advantage?"

"We could just stay here in this shed until the police arrive," Ethel said.

Sandra snickered, and it felt so good to laugh. She wrapped her arm around her son's waist, which was thick with extra fabric.

"No," Bob said firmly. "Though we'd be safe, I think I should go in and make sure everyone else is safe. And even though it feels warmer in here than it does outside, it's still too cold in here for you three to survive for very long."

Now that he mentioned it, Sandra's toes were incredibly cold.

"I think we should go inside," Bob said, "but I think we should sneak Peter in and stash him somewhere as warm as possible, so the killer doesn't know we found him. Then, we pretend to keep looking for him, while we *actually* try to figure out who the killer is."

Sandra clapped her hands together. "All right. Let's do it. My feet are cold."

Chapter 13

Bob sent his cohorts Sandra and Ethel in first, to make sure the coast was clear and to open the back door so that he could smuggle in a frozen ten-year-old. Then, under the cover of darkness, the three of them hustled Peter into the stinky props room.

"Agh!" Peter exclaimed. "What is that smell!"

"Old people church clothes," Ethel said, and Sandra laughed so loudly that Bob shushed her.

Peter looked at Ethel. "You don't smell like that!"

Ethel laughed. "Thank you! That's good news."

"Why don't you stay here with Peter," Bob said to Ethel.

"Yes!" Ethel held her giant flashlight up in the air. "If anyone comes this way, I will clobber him!"

"I'm going to lock you in," Bob said. "No one will come. But if you need to leave, you'll be able to open the door."

Ethel nodded stoically. Then she pulled a tote marked "Feathers" over and sat down. Sandra wondered what past production needed enough prop feathers to justify them getting their own tote.

"While you're here, would you guys mind looking around for Treasure's cell phone?" Sandra asked. "It's missing."

Peter looked around the room, wearing the same expression he always wore when she asked him to clean the litter box at home. "Mom, we're *never* going to find anything in here."

"Well, what else do you have to do but look?" She pointed at the bedding box. "And Ethel, there are blankets over there, if you get cold. They don't smell as bad as you might think, either." She looked at Bob. "So what's the plan for us?"

"Not sure." He opened the door for her and they both stepped out into the hallway. He softly shut the door behind them, and she stared at him, waiting for him to say something that would miraculously seal the door shut—probably something in Hebrew or Latin—but he didn't say anything at all. She was disappointed.

"Is it locked?"

"Yes." He seemed unaware of, or at least unconcerned with, her disappointment. "What do *you* think the plan should be?"

She shrugged. "First, I need to relight my candle." She thought for a second. "Then I think we should go ask people if they've seen Peter, and in the process, ask them other questions as well, like you said, sort of interrogating them without letting them know they're being interrogated."

"Hold out your candle."

She did, and instantly, the wick glowed with a yellow flame. "Thanks."

"You're welcome."

"Can you make my candle grow too? It's getting a bit stubby."

"It won't come to that."

What did that mean? That he couldn't do that particular miracle? Or that they would catch the killer before her candle burned out?

"Yes," he said. "I think that's a great plan. And don't be afraid to really provoke them. Maybe we can incite someone to try to grab you and stuff you in the shed."

She gasped. "You want to use me as bait?" She wasn't as horrified by that idea as she should have been.

He gave her an exasperated look. "I'll be right there. I won't let anything happen."

She wasn't as confident in his abilities as he was, but she didn't tell him that. "Okay, then, let's go." She took a step and then stopped. Go where? She had no idea where people were. She closed her eyes and strained to hear. At first, there was nothing, but then she thought she heard a bang from the green room, and she headed that way.

Bob followed closely behind, and soon they were both standing inside the green room, looking down at Gloria and her children, who were all huddled together under something that looked like a superhero cape.

"Wow, it really is warmer in here," Sandra said.

"Yes, I don't know why more people aren't in here," Gloria said.

"Because they're all out looking for Peter," Corina snapped, and Sandra felt guilty. Corina was scared for her friend, and Sandra was letting her worry for nothing, when he was safe and sound.

"Don't worry, Corina. I am confident that Peter is fine. I'm sure he just wandered off somewhere."

Corina looked skeptical. Maybe she knew Peter better than Sandra thought.

"When was the last time any of you saw him?" Sandra tried to get a conversation flowing, even though she knew none of these people were guilty of anything. As she talked, she wandered around the room, looking for the missing cell.

"We were all in the auditorium together when the lights went out," Gloria said. "I told the kids to stay put while I came down here to get Corina's phone for its flashlight. When I got here, I realized this was the warmest place to be, and I went back upstairs to get my kids. We've been here ever since. But I think he was still sitting in the auditorium when we left."

Corina nodded. "He was. And if we'd just stayed there, maybe he wouldn't be missing right now."

Oh, for heaven's sake. Sandra couldn't live like this. She crossed the room and dropped to one knee in front of Gloria. "I need to tell you a secret," she whispered.

"Don't!" Bob said firmly. "Didn't you say she *threatened* Treasure? She's our lead suspect!"

Sandra didn't think Gloria could wrestle Peter into a shed, and ignored Bob's protest. "You can't tell anyone else, but I've already found Peter."

"You did?" Corina cried.

At the same time, Sandra and Gloria shushed her, and Corina clamped a hand over her mouth. Her shocked expression gave way to relief and then to a glare directed at Sandra.

"Someone grabbed him, dragged him outside, and shoved him into the shed."

"There's a shed outside?" Gloria said, incredulous.

"Yes. It's a creepy little gardening shed. I'd never noticed it before either. Anyway, he's fine. He was a little scared and a little cold, but he's inside now, hiding. I don't know who took him, and I'm trying to figure it out, because, obviously, whoever took him also killed Treasure, and I don't want that person to know that I'm onto him. So please don't say anything to anyone. But!" She looked at Corina. "I know none of you guys pushed Treasure, and I didn't want to let Corina worry for nothing."

Corina's glare softened as her cheeks grew pink.

Sandra stood up. "So, I'll be going to continue my fake search. You guys can stay here—"

"No!" Gloria's eyes grew wide. "I don't think we're safe here if someone is snatching kids."

Sandra stopped. She really didn't think Gloria's kids were in danger, especially if Bob's theory was correct that the killer targeted Peter because of her. But how to convince them of that? "Um ... well, you can come with me, but I'm going to be traveling around actively looking for the killer, so I don't think you'd be much safer with me."

Gloria looked terrified, and Sandra's heart went out to her. She looked at the green room's door. "Does that lock?" No one answered her, so she walked back to the door to check. "It doesn't." She looked around the room. "Why don't you guys push some furniture in front of the door? That way no one can get in."

Gloria jumped up. "Great idea! Corban, help me push that table over to the door!"

"Wait, let us get out first!" Sandra said.

Gloria turned and stared at her. "Us? Are you planning to take one of us with you?"

"Um ... I mean me. Sorry, it's been a long day. Let *me* get out first. And kids, would you do me a favor while you wait for the police?"

They backed away from her, looking petrified.

"Would you look for a cell phone in here? Treasure's is missing."

They nodded eagerly. Not such a scary favor after all.

"If we find it, can I play with it?" Corban asked.

"Of course not," Gloria snapped.

"Sorry, Corban," Sandra said. "It will be evidence."

"Just like on NCIS?" His eyes grew bigger. She couldn't tell if he was scared or excited.

"Yes, just like on NCIS." She smiled at Gloria and then stepped out into the hallway, where she stayed until she heard Corban shoving the dresser in front of the door.

Chapter 14

Sandra found her next interrogee in the kitchen, rifling through the cupboards.

"What are you looking for?"

Matthew whirled around, looking guilty. "I'm starving," he said, with abnormal slowness.

Sandra crept closer to him and held her candle up to his face. His eyes were watery and bloodshot. "Are you stoned right now?"

He held a hand up to block the candle's faint light, as if it were blinding. "What's it to you?"

She lowered the candle. "Oh, wow, I don't know. There's a murderer running around, and I thought maybe you'd want to keep your mind sharp."

"I think better when I'm high." He sounded as if he actually believed this, and Sandra knew he wasn't a very good actor, so he probably did.

Either way, Sandra didn't want to argue with him. "Where were you when Treasure fell?"

"I don't know." He turned back toward the cupboards. "When did she fall?"

Sandra liked him less and less every second, and her opinion of him hadn't started out very high. She tried to be patient. "I don't know the exact time, but it had to have been minutes after she was rude to you on stage—"

"She wasn't rude to me."

Well, rude was a relative concept. Sandra thought. Just when *had* she fallen? It might be useful to pinpoint the time. She chewed on her lip as she stared at Matthew. She knew her gaze was making him uncomfortable, pot or no pot, and she thought this was a good thing. She hadn't heard Treasure fall. Wouldn't she have cried out? And those stairs were old and loud. During a play, cast had to tiptoe up and down them, or the audience could hear them. So surely it would have made some noise to fall down the stairs. Therefore, she must have fallen during the loud snowball fight scene, right? Otherwise, Sandra would have heard something. "She fell when the kids were rehearsing the snowball fight."

It was difficult to tell beneath his heavy eyelids, but she thought he glared at her. "I have no idea when that was. I was down here."

"She fell at about six-thirty. And *where* down here? In this kitchen?"

He looked around, as if he'd just realized he was in the kitchen. "I don't remember. Maybe the green room. Aren't you supposed to be looking for your son?"

She wanted to strangle him. Then there would be two killers on the loose. "Is that what you were looking for in the cupboards?"

His eyelids came up a little. Definitely a glare this time. "I know you think you're some sort of super detective because you got kidnapped once, but you're not. Why don't you just look for your kid, and let the cops catch the killer."

Bob put a hand on Sandra's shoulder. She'd forgotten he was there. She turned to look at him, and he jerked his head toward the door. He was right. Talking to Matthew was a waste of time. She turned to go, but then had a thought. "Matthew," she said, stopping and turning back for a second, "you must have been pretty angry when Treasure rejected you in front of everyone."

"Easy," Bob said, but Sandra wasn't scared of Matthew on his best day. And this wasn't his best day.

"She didn't reject me."

"She wasn't rude to you and she didn't reject you? Matthew, I *saw* it. She completely disrespected you. Didn't that make you angry? I would've been furious."

Matthew looked down at his hands. At first, he didn't respond, and when he did, his voice quavered. "That's just how she was."

Sandra couldn't believe it. He'd really cared about her? "Again, I'm sorry for your loss." Suddenly in a hurry to leave the young man in peace, she stepped out into the hallway and shut the door behind her.

"Well, that was weird," Bob said, "but I don't think he killed her. Now where do you want to go? Where is everyone?"

"Maybe they're back upstairs. But hang on. I want to go back to the green room."

"Why?"

She didn't answer him. She just walked to the green room. He'd find out soon enough. She tapped on the door. "Gloria?"

"Yes?"

"Still doing okay in there?"

There was a pause. "Define okay."

Okay was also a relative benchmark. "Still warm enough? And no one's trying to kill you?"

A faint giggle drifted through the door. "Yeah, then, I guess we're okay."

"Hey, do you know exactly when Treasure fell?"

Another pause. "No."

A meek little voice piped up. "I think she fell when we were doing the snowball scene," Corina said. "Because we didn't hear her."

Smart cookie. Maybe I should take her on the road. "Do you remember where you were during the snowball scene, Gloria?"

Again, a pause. Sandra leaned her forehead on the door and tried to be patient. "I'm not sure. I think I was in here."

Good. "Was Matthew in there with you?"

"No. No one was."

"Okay, thanks. You guys sit tight."

She stood up straight and looked at Bob. "So maybe he's not so innocent. He said he was in here."

"That doesn't mean much. Even *if* Gloria is telling the truth, her memory isn't foolproof."

A qualm wiggled its way into Sandra's brain. Why *hadn't* Gloria been upstairs watching the snowball scene? Both her kids were in it. What had she been doing instead?

Chapter 15

Sandra and Bob found Director Frank and ever-faithful Jan in the auditorium. Frank sat in the front row with his elbows on his knees and his head in his hands. Jan sat a few seats over from him, staring down at her candle, which was dripping hot wax onto her hands. It was a dismal scene. "Thanks for helping me look for my kid," Sandra said, and then instantly regretted it. Sarcasm never helped anything.

Neither of them acknowledged her presence. Had Bob made her invisible too? She looked at him for guidance, but he offered none.

She cleared her throat. Frank raised his eyes without raising his head. "Sorry about Peter." He paused, leaving her to wonder if he was going to say more. He did, finally. "This is a small theater, and Billy is looking. If he can be found, Billy will find him."

"What do you mean *if he can be found?*" Sandra asked.

Frank didn't answer.

"He means that he thinks the kid is already dead," Jan said, clearly believing the idea was preposterous.

Frank's head finally snapped up, and he shot eye-daggers toward his stage manager. Sandra wondered how many plays they'd done together. At least a hundred? "That is *not* what I meant, and don't put words in my mouth."

"You don't think he's in danger?" Sandra said to Jan.

She made a contemptuous *pfft* sound. "I told you what I think. The kid is probably hiding. Where's the girl? They're probably in the dark somewhere playing footsies."

Sandra stared at her. Just how old *was* Jan, anyway? "*Corina*," Sandra said slowly, "is in the green room with her mother, hiding, scared for her life, and worried sick about her *friend* Peter. How can you possibly be so sure that Peter hasn't been harmed, when there's a murder victim lying on the basement floor?"

"*I'm* not even sure she *is* a murder victim. I think the floozy fell down the stairs."

Sandra had difficulty not snickering at the word *floozy*.

"Let's not speak ill of the dead," Frank said. "Treasure had her attributes." Did he even believe himself?

"Yeah. Two of them," Jan said, pointing to her chest with both hands. Then she chuckled at her own joke.

Sandra wasn't sure what to make of it. She'd known Jan was grouchy, but this was something more. This was sociopathic behavior. "Are you just in denial?"

Jan grimaced, but Frank piped up, "I think that's it!" His eyes widened in excitement. "Thank you for figuring that out, Susan—"

"It's Sandra."

"Sorry, Sandra, I've been wondering what's wrong with her, even going so far as to be suspicious of her. *That's* why I've been sitting here, not out looking for your son. I thought if I kept her in my sights, the only person she could kill would be me. But I think you're assessment is more accurate. She *is* in denial. She's refusing to accept that this could happen or that it could happen *here*—"

"Stop psychoanalyzing me!" Jan bounded out of her chair and whirled to face him. "I am *not* in denial of anything!" She began to storm out of the room, and Sandra was keen to stop her. A suspect having no control over their emotions had to be a tactical advantage, didn't it?

"Jan, wait!"

Jan paused her stomping, but didn't turn back.

"Have either of you seen Treasure's cell phone?"

Bob gasped, and Sandra tried to ignore him. If he wanted to take over the questioning, he could do so at any time.

"No," Jan said, and started for the door again.

"Will you help me look?" Sandra asked, having no reason to ask it, but desperate to say something, anything, to keep Jan engaged.

She finally turned around. "Why would you want *my* help?" She looked at Frank. "He just accused me of murder. He's known me for forty years, and he just accused me of *murder*."

Sandra thought that detail was telling. She took a step toward Jan. "Jan, I think everyone is suspicious of everyone right now. I know it's hard, but don't be offended. And I don't know how, but I know you didn't kill Treasure." She knew no such thing, but it sounded good.

Jan's expression softened. It wasn't soft yet, but it was no longer flint. "What do you want with Treasure's phone?"

"I don't want anything with it, but I think it's suspicious that it's not on or near her body. So, maybe the murderer took it. Maybe if we find the phone, it will help us find the murderer."

"I'll help you look," Jan said decidedly.

"We've already checked the prop room!" Bob said quickly.

It took Sandra a second to realize why that was a fact worth spouting. Oh right. "We've already checked the prop room and the green room. It's not in either of those places." Sandra watched Jan walk away, unable to think of another way to stop her.

"I'll go help her look," Frank said, sans enthusiasm. He stood slowly, as if it hurt to do so, and then, head held high, shuffled away.

Sandra looked at Bob. "I don't think either of them did it. Peter said a man dragged him—"

"Jan smells a little manly."

"But is she hairy?" Sandra hadn't meant the question to be funny, but at the sound of it, she laughed. Bob didn't. "And I don't think Frank *could* drag Peter anywhere. He just had trouble getting out of his chair."

"I agree with you on that, but I'm still suspicious of Jan. Maybe there's more than one killer."

Sandra groaned. "Oh please, don't say that."

"Or maybe Jan killed Treasure and then got someone else to help kidnap Peter."

"That doesn't even make any sense. Who would help Jan? And why are you so stuck on Jan as the killer?"

He shrugged. "I don't like her."

"Angels are allowed to dislike people?"

Bob belted out a laugh. "Oh, of course. Don't be ridiculous." He started for the door. "Come on, let's follow them."

"But we still have to talk to Otis and Billy. Shouldn't we go look for them?"

"We'll do both."

Chapter 16

Sandra and Bob picked up Jan and Frank's trail and overheard Jan berating him in the office. "Why are you here? I am perfectly capable of looking for a cell phone on my own!" Sandra couldn't hear Frank's response, but he must have said something because Jan's ire increased. "Go look in another room! Get away from me! If you don't buzz off, I'm not going to help look!"

Bob looked at Sandra with one eyebrow cocked. His silent expression said, *I told you so.*

Sandra still wasn't convinced. If Jan had killed someone, wouldn't she be doing a better job of acting innocent?

Frank came out of the office, started when he saw Sandra, and then headed down the stairs.

"I think we should stay with her," Bob said.

Sandra was not surprised to hear that this was the plan. For several minutes, they stood stupidly in the hallway doing nothing, waiting for Jan to search the small office.

Suddenly, Bob said, "I'm going in," and vanished.

Sandra leaned against the wall to wait and flinched when the wall creaked beneath her weight.

Just when she was sure the police would arrive before Jan ever left the office, Bob appeared in front of her, grabbed her forearm, and yanked her into the shadows. Then he peeked around the corner. "She's coming out," he narrated. "And she just went into the concessions booth." He vanished again.

This was stupid. She was wasting her time waiting for Bob to spy on someone who was not the killer, someone who was actually trying to help. She needed to find Otis and Billy. They'd said they would go look for Peter outside, but surely they weren't still out there? They'd be Popsicles by now. She decided to check everywhere inside before venturing out to look for them, partly because she was sure they were back inside by now and partly because she didn't want to go out in the storm.

She went back through the auditorium, which was still empty, and down the treacherous back stairs. She rechecked the kitchen and found Frank shining a flashlight into the refrigerator. "Hungry?"

He looked at her as if she were stupid. "No, I'm looking for that blasted phone."

Oh yeah. She'd just told him to do that, hadn't she? "Right. Of course. I was just kidding. Have you seen Otis or Billy?"

He shook his head. "Sorry, no. I haven't seen anyone since I saw you upstairs."

"All right. Thanks for your help." Sandra left the kitchen and headed for the costume room, wondering why they hadn't thought to look there first. What a great place to hide something, with all those pockets.

Her stomach sank when she saw Jan with her hand on the doorknob of the props room. Bob stood right beside her.

"Why is this locked?" Jan snapped when she saw Sandra. "This can't be locked! This is never locked! We don't even have a key!"

"Uh ..."

"You said you searched it! Did you lock it?"

"Maybe? I'm sorry, it was an accident."

"Accident?" Jan screeched. "How can you accidentally lock a door? The phone could be in there! Your son could be in there! We need to open this door!" She was screaming now, and as Sandra stepped closer, she could see that the woman's face was as red as a lobster. Was she going to have a heart attack?

"Maybe we should sit down for a minute." Sandra reached for Jan's elbow, but she yanked it away from her.

"I don't need to sit down! I need to search the props room!" Still screeching.

"Jan, I'm concerned about you. I can't imagine how stressful this must be—"

"You have *no idea* how stressful this is. You don't know anything about me, or what I've done for this theater." Her voice cracked, and she turned to stare at the door. "I would do anything for this place," she said softly, and though Sandra felt bad that Jan was crying, she was so grateful that the screaming had stopped.

She put a hand on her back. "I'm so sorry, Jan. Really, let's go sit down for a minute. Maybe if we talk this out together, we can figure out—"

"I don't want to talk anything out with you!" Back to screeching. "What I want is to search this prop closet!" She pounded on the door, and for one panicked moment, Sandra worried Ethel might open it.

Sandra stood there, frozen. What should she do? She looked to Bob for help, but he also looked stymied. They were being steamrolled, and Sandra felt powerless to stop it.

Otis emerged from the shadows, no longer wearing the "extra layers" he'd borrowed from the prop room. Good, she'd been right. He wasn't outside looking anymore. "What's wrong, Jan?" He put a hand on her shoulder, and she let him. Absurdly, Sandra felt a pang of jealousy. Why did Jan like Otis and not her?

In a normal volume, Jan explained, "Someone took Treasure's cell phone. I am looking for it." Her words came out staccato. Sandra had never heard her talk like that. Otis stared at her as if trying to read her, but before he could say anything, Jan said, "Go away. I'll find it. You go look for the *boy*."

Otis stood there staring for another several seconds, and then walked away.

Sandra turned to follow him, leaving Bob to deal with Jan and the locked door. "Otis, wait up!" She jogged up the stairs to catch him. "Have you seen any signs of Peter? I sure do appreciate that you're helping to look."

He gave her that same weird stare, as if he was trying to peer into her mind. Did *he* suspect *her*? Is that what was happening here? Was he staring into her eyes in hopes of seeing a flicker of guilt? Why on earth would she hide her own son? Oh wait, she *had* hid her own son, hadn't she?

"Sorry, nothing yet. But I'll keep looking." He turned and started up the stairs.

"Where have you looked?"

He paused and looked back over his shoulder. "Pardon?"

"Where have you looked already? So I'll know where to look."

He paused for too long. How could he not know where he'd looked? Maybe he hadn't looked at all. "I've looked everywhere," he finally said. Oh, so maybe he'd been trying to think of a place he *hadn't* looked. That made sense.

"So where are you going to look now?"

He shrugged one shoulder as he turned to go up the stairs again. "Guess I'm going to start over."

She couldn't think of anything else to ask him, so she let him get a head start. She still followed him, in case she thought of something intelligent to say, but she gave him enough buffer to keep him from realizing she was tailing him. She hoped. As she watched him duck into the concessions booth, the outside door opened just feet to her left, scaring the absolute tar out of her.

In blew frigid air, fat pinging raindrops, and Billy.

"Hey, Sandra," he said, sounding resigned, as he shook the ice out of his hair.

She couldn't believe it. "Why are you still out there!?"

He looked around in all directions, and then grabbed her arm and pulled her to him. Her breath caught. He looked into her eyes with the gravest expression in his, and said, "I found something and I'm afraid it's not good."

Chapter 17

"What?" Sandra asked. "What did you find?"

Billy looked around furtively. "It looks like someone went into the shed against their will, as if they had been *forced* to go in there."

Sandra tried to fake surprise and was pretty sure she failed. "Oh?"

He nodded. "I thought I'd found Peter, but the shed was empty."

She waited for him to say more. "What do you think that means?"

He let go of her arm and held his hands out with his palms up. "Not sure. But it scares me. Did someone put Peter in there? And if they then took him out, where did they put him? Or maybe he got out and ran for help? But that's not good either. There's no house for a mile in any direction, and it's way too cold for him to be out there for too long."

She nodded, trying to look scared. "Thank you for staying outside so long. You didn't have to risk freezing to death. You should've come in when Otis did."

Billy's brows fell in confusion. "Otis?"

"Yeah, didn't he go outside to look with you?"

Billy rubbed his chin. "I don't remember. I guess he might have. But he didn't go *with* me. He must have gone off on his own to look."

That didn't make sense.

"I got to say, Sandra, you're taking this awfully well. My wife would be having a full-blown panic attack by now." He gave a loud, humorless chuckle.

"I'm really trying to keep it together."

"Well, you're doing a good job. I'll keep looking, but I lost feeling in my feet, so I came inside for a bit. I'll head back out as soon as I'm sure I'm not going to lose my toes. But I checked every car and every trunk out there, and he wasn't in them."

"How did you check the trunks?"

Billy pulled a crowbar out of his oversized coat. "I'll pay to have them fixed, but if he was in one of them, I didn't want to waste time asking for keys." He drew a long breath. "Now that I mention it, maybe my toes aren't so important. I think I'll head back out now."

"Billy, wait." She *had* to tell him. She looked around, just like he had minutes before. "Let's go into the office." She opened the door slowly, afraid a cat or a clown was going to jump out at her, and then they stepped inside. She shut the door behind him and then looked up at him. "Billy, I owe you a huge apology." She didn't know where to start. "I'm so sorry, and so embarrassed. You probably heard about what happened to me in the fall, with the soccer refs? Well, I guess now I think I'm some sort of detective or something, because I've been scheming and trying to figure this thing out, but I didn't stop to think about how me pretending to be a detective would affect other—"

He put a firm hand on her shoulder. "You're not making any sense. Maybe you're not handling this as well as I thought." He pulled out a chair and gently pushed her into it, making her feel even guiltier. "Here, take a load off. Whatever you think you have to apologize for, can it wait till we find Peter?"

"No!" she said sharply. She wheeled her chair to the left and pulled another chair toward him. "Please, sit."

He looked reluctant, but he sat.

She took a deep breath. She really didn't want to admit this. "Please don't hate me, but I already found Peter, and he's fine."

Billy leaned away from her so abruptly that his chair wheeled backward.

"I'm so sorry, Billy. When we found him, I totally forgot that you'd even gone outside, and then it never occurred to me that you'd still be out there ... so, anyway, I thought that if I didn't let the killer know that—"

"You said *we* found him?" he interrupted. "Who else knows?" She'd never seen Billy look angry. It wasn't a good look for him.

"Ethel."

He chuckled. "Well, it's hard to be mad at Ethel, now, isn't it? Where was he?"

"You were right. He was in the shed."

"He's not hurt? He didn't get too cold?"

She shook her head. "He's fine. But I made him and Ethel hide in the prop room."

Billy scrunched up his face. "It smells awful in there." He rubbed his chin for several seconds and then looked at her. "I guess it's hard to be mad at you too. I can see where you were going with it."

She was incredulous. And beyond grateful. She thought about giving Billy a giant hug, but that would be awkward, and he was all wet. "You can?"

"Sure, sure. Did Peter see who grabbed him?"

"No."

"Oh, well, but maybe the killer thinks he might have seen something. So if you let the killer think he's still got the kid stashed, then he still thinks he's got the upper hand."

She let out a long breath. "Exactly. I was trying to be all smart and conniving, but I'm not very good at it—"

"Oh no, I think you are pretty good at it." He slapped his thighs and then stood. "So, if you don't need me to look for Peter, how else can I help?"

"I don't know. Who do *you* think did it? I mean, none of these people seem like killers." She almost told him that Bob suspected Jan, but caught herself just in time.

He looked contemplative. "My money's on Matthew. He had the hots for her, and she rejected him. Plus, he's weird."

"And he's high as a kite right now."

Billy guffawed. "Really? Where is he?"

"Don't know."

"Well, maybe that's what I can do to help. Just stick to him like glue, so if he tries anything goofy, I can be there to stop it."

"Would you?" she was so appreciative she thought she might cry. She was forming quite a team of crime fighters. As long as none of her team members was the killer.

Chapter 18

Sandra laid her cheek against the green room's door. "You guys doing okay in there?"

Corina's response came immediately. "I have to go to the bathroom."

Sandra waited for more information, but none came. "Gloria? Do you want me to take her?"

"Absolutely not. She can either hold it or go in here." She sounded exhausted and terrified. "We're not coming out, and we're not letting anyone else in."

"Anyone else? Why, did someone try to get in?"

"Yes," Gloria whispered. "Matthew. He said it was warm in here, but it's not that warm anymore."

"Did he try to force his way in?"

"No. He just begged."

"Good." Sandra looked up and down the dark hallway. "You guys are doing well. Did you find the phone?"

"No."

She said it so quickly that Sandra wondered if they'd really looked, but how could she nag them about that? "Are you still looking?"

"No." Another quick negative.

Sandra tried to think of a way to be tactful and couldn't so she decided tact was unnecessary right now. "Did you do a thorough job? We really need to find it. Have you looked everywhere?"

"Yes!" Gloria's voice was closer to the door now. "And I really don't give a rat's buttock about that stupid phone."

Sandra tried not to be annoyed, and failed. "Even if it lets us catch the killer?"

Gloria snorted. "Catch him? What are you going to do with him then? What good does it do to catch him? Won't that only make him mad?"

While Sandra was trying to figure out a way to respond to that, Bob appeared beside her with wet hair and flushed cheeks. She hadn't known angels could get flushed cheeks. "I found it!" He opened his palm to reveal a giant iPhone in a bejeweled hot pink case.

Sandra gasped. "Where was it?"

"Where was what?" Gloria asked from the other side of the door.

"Uh ... nothing. Sorry."

"Come on, let's go to the prop room," Bob said.

She couldn't get there fast enough. Bob opened the door as if it had never been locked, and then Sandra stared around the room in wonder. It had been a mess before. Now it looked like a cyclone's ground zero. "Uh ... what happened here?"

"Sorry," Peter whispered, not looking the least bit sorry, his left hand full of ropes of varying sizes. "I've been looking for the phone."

"In the rope box?" Bob asked.

Peter shrugged. "Seemed as good a place as any." Despite her near-rabid curiosity about where Bob had found the phone, Sandra did pause to appreciate her son's ingenuity.

Bob held up the phone. "You don't need to look anymore."

Ethel rushed over to peer at the phone. Peter folded the top of the rope box shut and sat down on it.

"Where was it?" Sandra asked impatiently. She was considering throttling an angel.

"Outside." Bob looked around for a seat and then rearranged some totes to fashion himself a perch.

"Tell us!" Sandra almost-hollered.

He grinned mischievously. "Okay. So, I watched Jan find it. And it was weird. She found it in the sound booth, and she seemed surprised to find it. It was clear she hadn't hidden it there. It was also clear she was greatly relieved to find it. She immediately tucked it into the waistband of her pants and then sneaked outside.

Sandra tried, but she couldn't picture Jan sneaking anywhere.

"I followed her outside. She shuffled all the way across the lawn, only falling once, and then she—"

"She fell?" Ethel asked, her voice sweet with concern.

"Yes. For a minute, I thought I'd have to rescue her, but she managed to get herself upright and then she continued toward the drop-off on the side of the lawn."

Sandra again tried to visualize what Bob was describing, but she didn't know about any drop off. The lawn was huge, and she could believe, in this mountainous terrain, that there was indeed a drop-off at the edge of it.

"And then she wound back and threw the phone into the woods."

"Over the edge?" Peter asked.

"Over the edge."

They all took a few seconds to absorb that.

"Why would she do that?" Sandra asked.

"It's a good thing you were the one to go get it," Peter mused. "It would've taken me forever. I'm not even sure I'd be able to climb back up here."

"Yes, I admit that I didn't do much climbing."

"Why would she throw the phone away?" Sandra asked again. She didn't give a hoot about how difficult it would be for a human to climb back up the mountain. That was why she'd invited an angel to assist her investigation.

"I have no idea," Bob said.

Sandra held her hand out. "Can I look at it?"

Bob handed it over. The phone was still on, though the battery was low. Sandra wasn't surprised by this. It seemed reasonable that Treasure would put a hurting on her phone battery, especially out here in the willywacks where there was no signal. She scrolled through recent messages, hoping to find something interesting, but found nothing of note. She did notice that Treasure didn't have a lot of female contacts. She opened the photo gallery and gasped.

"What?" Peter asked.

Sandra's cheeks got hot, and she hoped people wouldn't notice in the dim light. She looked up at Bob. "There's a photo ..." Words failed her.

"Of?"

She handed the phone back to him, and he looked down at the screen. "Oh dear."

"Exactly."

He swiped the screen with his thumb. "Oh dear," he said again. He swiped again. "Oh my."

"The third one got an 'oh my' instead of an 'oh dear,'" Ethel said. "That one must be a doozy."

Sandra snickered. "I only saw the first one, and I wish I could burn it out of my brain. I'm afraid it may be lodged there till the day I die."

"What is it?" Peter asked. "Is she naked?"

Bob nodded. "And she's not alone." He turned the screen off and looked up at everyone. "But the man in the pictures isn't anyone here, so I don't think the pictures are related."

"But there must be something incriminating on the phone, or Jan wouldn't have thrown it off a cliff," Sandra said.

Bob nodded. "I'll keep looking at it. And in the meantime, we need to keep a close eye on Jan. She's obviously involved."

"It wasn't Jan who dragged me to the shed."

"Are you sure?" Sandra asked. "Jan is a strong woman." She'd seen her move giant sets like they were made of paper.

Doubt flickered across his face. "I don't think so. Maybe she smells like a man. I've never sniffed her. But I doubt she has hairy arms."

"That's it!" Bob bounced to his feet.

"What's it?" Sandra asked, after giving him time to elaborate.

"As strange as it sounds, I think we need to go around and let Peter sniff people."

Chapter 19

"Good news!" Sandra announced to Frank, who was in the office, looking at a pile of paperwork. How he could read anything in the meager candlelight was beyond her. Maybe he wasn't reading. Maybe he was just trying to stay busy. Or maybe he was just trying to *look* busy.

Frank glanced up, looked at Peter, and, without looking the least bit relieved to see him alive and well, asked, "Where was he?"

Though Bob had instructed her to tell people that Peter had just wandered off after all, Sandra blurted out the truth. "Someone stuffed him in the shed outside." She stepped into the small office and went to stand behind the seated Frank. "Step into his light," she said to Peter, "so I can get a look at you." This ruse didn't even make sense, as Sandra held a candle of her own.

Still, Peter stepped uncomfortably close to Frank and was hardly subtle as he took a big sniff.

His personal space invaded, Frank tried to push away from Peter, but his chair didn't move an inch before hitting Sandra. "What is this about?"

Peter stuck out his hand. "Thank you for looking for me."

Without telling the kid that he hadn't worked very hard to find him, Frank took Peter's offered hand and shook it.

As they shook, Peter roughly wrapped his hand around Frank's right wrist and tried to shove his sleeve up. Sandra knew this wouldn't work, and it didn't. The sport coat sleeve slid up a few inches, but the dress shirt beneath it was buttoned up tight as a drum. Frank yanked his hand out of Peter's grip, and flew out of his chair. He quickly distanced himself from the intruders and pressed his body against the wall, completely out of the light from his candle. "I ask again, what is this about?"

"We just wanted to tell you that we found him, and that he's all right. Let's go, Peter."

Her son completely ignored her. "Mr. Flamatti, may I please see your arm?"

"I beg your pardon?"

Peter picked Frank's candle up off the desk and stepped closer to the director. "I'm sorry, but I'm trying to figure out if you're the one who shoved me in that shed, and I need to see your arm."

Peter had decided to simply tell the truth. An odd tactical maneuver, but worth a shot.

Frank stood still for several seconds and then wordlessly, with great poise, took off his sport coat, unbuttoned his sleeve, and then neatly rolled it up. He held it out toward Peter, who patted his arm as one would pat a cat he didn't know well. Then Peter looked at his mom. "It's not him."

"Of course not," Frank said evenly as he started to put himself back together.

"Thank you," Sandra said. "We'll get out of your hair now." Not realizing she'd sort of made a pun until it was out of her mouth, she hurried out of the room before she could laugh, shooing Peter out in front of her.

"I'm going, I'm going," he said, annoyed with her.

She shut the door behind them and stopped moving so she could decide where to go next.

"Let's find Billy," he said.

"It wasn't Billy."

"How do you know?"

"I just do."

Bob appeared beside her.

"Where have you been? I thought you were going to go with us. Peter walking around smelling people was your plan!"

"I know, but I wanted to go see where the police are."

Oh! What a good idea! Why hadn't she thought of that? "And where are they?"

"They're still miles away. They're following a sand truck. There are no other cars on the road."

Everyone else knew enough to stay home.

"Where is Ethel?" Bob asked.

"She's still in the props room. She says she's too exhausted to go on a scent tour—"

"I'll go check on her." Bob disappeared, but was back in a single second.

"Was she still there?" Sandra asked, though she was certain of the answer.

"Yes, wrapped in a blanket, staring at the door, and clutching that flashlight like it was a rifle."

Sandra snickered at the image. "Any idea how much longer it will take for the police to get here?"

He shook his head slowly. "Maybe just under an hour?"

Bummer. "Then I guess we need to keep sniffing."

"It wasn't Frank?" Bob asked.

"No," Peter said, sounding too serious for a ten-year-old. "I need to sniff Billy."

Bob chuckled. "All right. Let's go find him, then." He led them into the auditorium, but Billy wasn't there. They turned around and returned to the front of the building, where they checked the sound room, the concessions booth, the office, and the restrooms.

No dice.

"He must be downstairs," Sandra said, annoyed that they were spending precious time looking for the most innocent man in the theater.

"Let's go check," Bob said after starting down the steps.

Billy Adams was sitting at the kitchen table eating from a box of Girl Scout cookies. "Want some?" he asked when Sandra traipsed in. Then he saw Peter. "All right, my man! Good to see your mum sprung you!" He shoved an entire cookie in his mouth and crunched loudly.

Bob looked at her suspiciously.

"I told him that we were hiding Peter."

"Why?" Bob cried, his voice dripping with accusation.

"Because he was outside looking for him! He was going to die of hypothermia looking for a kid who wasn't missing!"

"Uh, Mom? You're not making any sense." Peter's eyes were huge.

Oh *shoot*. Not only did she appear to Billy to be talking to her imaginary friend, she was *fighting* with him. She looked at Billy. "I'm sorry. I'm feeling a little out of sorts."

Billy was still holding the box of cookies out toward them. "They're a little stale, but will do in a pinch."

"This is indeed a pinch," Sandra said, trying to offer some levity.

Finally taking the hint that no one wanted to share his old cookies, Billy pulled the box back to his chest and reached in for another dose of Do-si-dos. She pulled a chair away from the table and sat down beside him. She nodded toward the chair across from her. "Have a seat, Peter."

He looked down at the table, where Billy had a flashlight and a cell phone.

"Does that phone have a light?" Peter asked.

"A-yup."

"Could I borrow the flashlight then?" Peter held his empty hands out to his sides. "I'm lightless, depending on my mom's pathetic candle."

Billy laughed, and a few cookie crumbs flew out of his mouth. "Sure! Help yourself. Now that I don't need to look for you anymore, I don't need the backup."

Peter grabbed the flashlight and sat down, leaning ridiculously close into Billy on his way down, so much so that Billy pushed himself back against his chair. Peter's eyes widened as he inhaled through his nose and he looked at Sandra with big eyes.

Don't be ridiculous. If her son named Billy as his kidnapper, she really wouldn't know whether to believe him. She shook her head slightly.

He looked at Billy. "Could I see your arm?"

Billy laughed. "What?"

"Peter, it's not him. He nearly froze to death outside looking for you."

"Exactly," Peter said to her and then looked at Billy. "Could I just see your arm, please?"

Billy held it out in front of him.

"Can you push up your sleeve, please?"

Sandra thought she might die from the awkwardness.

Billy blinked, obviously confused, and then pushed his sleeve up to his elbow and held out his arm.

Chapter 20

Billy's arm was nearly hairless. Sandra sighed in relief. Then she slapped the table and stood. "Let's go, Peter."

"Huh?" Billy said. "Someone want to tell me what's going on?"

She opened her mouth to answer him, but Peter shook his head wildly, his eyes wide.

"I'll explain later," she said. "Sorry to be weird." Then she headed for the door, with Peter close on her tail.

They were barely out in the hallway when Bob said, "That was him?"

Peter chewed on his lip. "I don't know."

"What does that mean?"

"His arm wasn't hairy," Sandra said and started down the hall.

"But he *did* smell the same," Peter said, not following her.

"Come on, we've still got to sniff Matthew and Otis," Sandra said, and then realized she had said that far too loudly. Those two could be anywhere, and she couldn't imagine what they might think if they heard her say such a thing.

"Matthew just went into the bathroom," Bob said. "I don't know where Otis is."

As if summoned, Matthew appeared at the end of the hallway. "Hi, Matthew!" Sandra tried to sound excited. "We found Peter!"

"Great," Matthew said, making the word three syllables long.

Before Sandra realized what was happening, Peter was standing right next to Matthew, sniffing his hair. As soon as he did so, he recoiled and slapped a hand over his mouth.

"Dude!" Matthew said, indignant. "What was that for?"

"Sorry," Peter mumbled as he scurried back to Sandra's side.

She tried not to laugh. Matthew was the only one not wearing long sleeves, and she got her candle as close to his skin as she could. It looked like a normal man's arm, not particularly hairy. She looked to Peter for confirmation, but he appeared to be too horrified for further investigation.

"Have you seen Otis?" she asked Matthew.

"Who's Otis?" He closed his eyes and scrunched up his face. "Oh, you mean Grandpa?"

Sandra took a deep breath. "Yes, I mean Grandpa."

His eyelids lifted a millimeter. "Ah, no, I haven't seen him in a while. Why, where is he?"

"I just heard something backstage," Bob said.

Good. Sandra was glad to have a reason to stop talking to Matthew. "Okay, let's go backstage then."

"Let's take the back stairs," Bob said. "It's a lot quicker."

"I'd rather not." Sandra didn't want to force her son to skirt a dead body. It was bad enough she was dragging him around like a cop's bloodhound.

"Fine. I'll meet you there." Bob headed for the back of the building while Sandra turned toward the front.

They were barely out of Matthew's earshot when Peter said, "Why did he smell like a skunk?"

"I'll explain later," Sandra said. She would be explaining a lot of things later. They hurried up the stairs and down the aisle of the auditorium toward the stage. Sandra felt a new sense of urgency. If none of the other men had hairy arms, then Otis must be their guy, right? She couldn't picture it, though. He was a grouch, for sure, but a kidnapper? She didn't think so. His wife was too sweet to be married to a murderer. Besides, he was a little old to be dragging a preteen through a blizzard.

They found him sitting on a short stool in a dark corner backstage. Bob stood nearby.

"Ah!" Otis cried when Peter shined his new flashlight on him. He held a hand up to shield his eyes. "Point that thing somewhere else!"

"What are you doing back here?" Sandra asked.

"Trying to avoid social interaction," he said pointedly.

"Why are you sitting in the dark?"

He tipped his head back. "What is there back here that I need to see?"

Sandra nodded toward Otis, trying to urge Peter to go take a sniff. He looked hesitant. Otis was shoved so far into the corner that it would be difficult to discreetly get close to him. And Otis had made it clear that he didn't *want* anyone to get close to him—discreetly or not. But she was completely out of patience. "Just do it!"

"Do what?" Otis asked, immediately suspicious.

Wearing his I-really-don't-want-to-eat-this-Brussels-sprout-face, Peter took a quick step toward the man and leaned in for a sniff.

Not surprisingly, Otis jerked away from him, but the walls stopped him from getting far. He opened his mouth to lambaste the impertinent child leaning over him, but before he could get a word out, Peter said, "Could I please see your arm?"

"What?! No!" Otis stood up abruptly, and Peter staggered back from him.

Otis pushed past Sandra, but she reached out and grabbed his arm, surprising herself with her assertiveness. "Please, Otis. It's important."

His expression softened a little, but then he looked at Peter and his grimace returned. "Why does he want to see my arm?"

"We're trying to clear you from suspicion," Sandra said, with an attempt to sound gentle.

Otis's eyes widened. "Why? Did Treasure claw someone on her way down?"

Sandra frowned. She hadn't even thought of that. That would make sense, wouldn't it? Never mind the hairiness; she should've been checking for scratches. Now they were going to have to make another round. "Maybe, yes. Would you mind?"

Now seeming *overly* compliant, Otis pushed both his sleeves up, and then held his arms out for inspection. Peter shined his flashlight on them, and then Otis flipped them over.

No scratches, and very little hair.

"There. Satisfied?" He pulled his sleeves back down. "Now, I'm going to go try to find some solitude in this godforsaken place. Please, leave me be."

A pang of sorrow shot through Sandra's heart. This poor man. "Of course. Sorry to have bothered you."

He flicked his flashlight on and disappeared around a corner.

Sandra looked at Bob. "Now what?"

Bob shook his head. "I have no idea." He looked at Peter. "What did he smell like?"

"He smelled just like Billy."

"Really?" Sandra didn't know what to make of this. "As in they use the same aftershave?"

Peter shrugged. "I don't know." He looked like he was about to burst into tears. "Or the same deodorant, or the same laundry detergent." He collapsed onto Otis's stool. "I don't know," he said again, and then the tears came.

Chapter 21

"Are you sure that your abductor's arms were hairy?" Bob asked.

"Give him a break," Sandra said, her hackles raised. "He's overwhelmed."

Bob gave her a patronizing look. "I can see he's upset, but this is a pressing matter." He looked down at Peter and repeated the question.

Peter put his head in his hands and mumbled, "I don't know. I thought so." They all stayed quiet for nearly a minute, until Peter looked up and said, "Yes. I'm sure of it. They were *so* hairy. It grossed me out. I grabbed the hair and twisted, trying to hurt him."

"And did it?" Bob asked.

"Did it what?"

"Did it hurt him?"

Peter looked contemplative. "I don't know. I was doing a lot of things at the same time to try to hurt him."

"And he didn't make any sounds?"

Peter thought about that for a few seconds. "He didn't say anything, but he did grunt a little. But it was quiet, like he had his hand over his mouth or something—"

"Like it was muffled?" Sandra said.

He looked at her. "Yeah, kinda."

She looked at Bob. "Maybe he was wearing a mask!"

Bob nodded. "That would make sense. It's cold out there. Maybe we need to look for a ski mask—"

"Not a *ski* mask! We're in a theater! I mean a *mask* mask."

Bob's face was blank. He obviously was the sports angel, *not* the theater angel.

"Come on! I have an idea!" Sandra took off for the front stairs, assuming they'd follow. She was moving so fast that halfway down the stairs, her candle went out. This wasn't exactly a surprise. It had already melted down to a nub. She stopped and waited for Peter and Bob to catch up. Once Peter's light reached her feet, she got going again.

"Where are we going?" Bob asked, but she didn't want to expend the energy it would take to explain.

She hurried down the hall and then paused in front of the costume room door. She looked both ways to make sure no one was watching. They were on the brink of solving this thing, and she didn't want the killer to know. No one was watching, so she ripped open the door and ushered them inside before closing it behind them.

"That's it!" Peter cried, too loudly.

"I thought it might be," Sandra said, feeling quite proud of herself.

"What's it?"

Peter shined his light around the room, breathing deeply through his nose. "What *is* that?"

"What are you talking about? What is what?" Bob was losing patience.

"The smell. It's the same smell as Billy and Otis."

"I don't know what it is," Sandra said to Peter. "It's some kind of soap smell. Shine your light over here." She headed for the far corner. "I have an idea."

Peter followed her with his light.

"Come here." She reached the pile of animal costumes and picked up the top one. Sure enough, it was damp. "It's wet!" she exclaimed. She held it up so Peter could see it.

He reached out and touched it, and then yanked his hand away as if it had stung him. "Yeah, that's it."

Sandra dropped the furry monstrosity back onto the pile.

"Is that a *bear* costume?" Bob asked.

The costume had a small straw hat sewn onto the top. "*Smokey* the Bear costume, I think," Sandra said. "And when I saw Billy come in from outside, he was wearing a giant red plaid coat. It was huge on him. I wonder if he took it from in here, because it was warmer than the coat he'd worn tonight."

Bob, suddenly twenty feet away from them, held up a green box. "Or the man just uses Irish Spring soap." Bob brought the box closer to Peter, who didn't even need to lean in to smell it.

"Yeah, that's definitely the smell."

"You know what this means," she said.

"That Peter's kidnapper wants to prevent forest fires?"

She laughed. "Look at the angel being funny."

Something like pride flickered across Bob's face, but then vanished.

"It means that we still don't know if it was Billy or Otis who grabbed me," Peter said. "Either one of them could have put on that costume."

"It means more than that," Sandra said. "It means it could have been a woman."

Peter groaned. "I am *not* going around smelling all the women."

"You don't have to, now that we know what the smell is. We can let Bob do it."

"Me?" Bob looked incredulous.

"Yes, *you*. You're the only one of us who's invisible. Invisible sniffers are far less obvious, and far less rude."

"Angels don't have a very good sense of smell," he tried.

"And angels aren't supposed to lie, either."

He closed his eyes. "Fine. I'll do it. Let's—"

A scream sounded through the walls, sending an icy shiver down Sandra's spine.

Bob vanished.

Chapter 22

Peter got to the costume room's door before Sandra did and reached for the handle. He twisted it, pushed, and then twisted the other way and pushed again. "It's locked."

"Shine your light on the doorknob."

Peter did, and she turned the small lock. Then she turned the knob and pushed.

Nothing happened.

"Told you. It's locked."

She didn't see how this was possible. She turned the button the opposite way and pushed. Still nothing. She took the flashlight out of his hand.

"Hey!" he protested.

She scooched down to examine the lock as she turned the knob. From this viewpoint, she could clearly see the latch bolt sliding in and out. The door wasn't locked. But it wasn't opening either. Someone must have put something against it on the outside. She stood up straight. "Maybe Bob locked us in."

"Why would he do that?"

She had no idea. "To protect us, maybe?"

"But wouldn't he tell us?"

"I would think so, but he was in a hurry to see what that scream was about." Trouble was, *she* wanted to see what the scream was about too. She turned the handle, lowered her shoulder, and drove her body into the door. This did nothing to the door and hurt her shoulder.

"Let me try." Peter pushed her aside with this hip. He tried the same exact maneuver and got the same exact results. Then he stared at the door as if it had offended him. "We're trapped."

"He must have locked us in." She wasn't sure this was true, but it was more comforting than the alternative.

She tried to act nonchalantly. She didn't want Peter to know that their current situation was killing her. It wasn't that she was afraid of the killer, and it wasn't that she was afraid of being locked in an Irish Spring factory: it was killing her not to know who had screamed and why. There was action on the other side of the door, and she, Sandra the secret sleuth, was missing out. "You're Mr. Soccer. Can you kick it down?"

His eyes widened with excitement, and her maternal instinct overrode her curiosity. "Don't kick too hard. I don't want you to hurt yourself."

He backed up a few paces and then stared at the door for so long she wondered if he wasn't going to try it.

"You don't have to, you know."

"No, I will. I want to. I'm just trying to think *how* to do it. Kicking a door is nothing like kicking a ball. It's more like karate. And I don't know karate."

The kid had a point. "You're right. Maybe it's a bad idea."

"No! I want to do it." He backed up a few more steps, and then started running toward the door. Just before he reached it, he abruptly turned away and walked back to where he'd started.

"It was a bad idea. I was just brainstorming. You don't have to do this—"

"Stop saying that," he growled.

It occurred to her that in his mind, his manhood might be on the line. Again, he started running, and then just before he reached the door, he let out a weird grunt and leapt into the air with one leg outstretched. She braced herself for the contact he would feel, but it never happened. The door flew open just before his foot connected, and he fell to the floor, smashing his bony hip into the threshold. "Ahh!" he cried out, and she rushed to his side.

"Sorry," Bob said. "Didn't know you were flying there."

Peter sat up and pushed his mother away. "I'm fine."

She helped him up anyway and then looked at Bob. "Did you lock us in?"

He took the flashlight out of her hand and shined it toward a shim of wood lying near the wall. "No. Someone shoved that under the door." He looked at her. "Whoever the bad guy is here, they're getting worried about your progress."

"What progress?" she whispered. "We know less than we did an hour ago."

"Yes, but they don't know that."

After one more glance to make sure Peter was okay after his first failed karate kick, she asked, "Who screamed?"

"Jan." Bob sounded disappointed.

"Is she okay?"

"Yes. She saw a mouse."

"You're kidding."

"No. The theater cat obviously isn't doing its job."

"He's probably cuddled up somewhere trying to stay warm."

"Where was she?" Peter asked.

"Who? The cat?" Bob said. "I thought it was a boy."

"No, not the cat. Jan!" Peter was exasperated with Bob, angelic being or not.

"Oh. She was in the kitchen."

"So then we do know more than we used to," Peter said thoughtfully.

"Oh yeah? What do we know?" Sandra asked.

"It wasn't Jan. She was too far away to lock us in here. And we know it wasn't Matthew. I would've been able to smell him through any costume. That dude stinks. I don't think it was Frank, because he didn't smell like the soap. And we know it's not Ethel. So it was either Otis, Billy, or Gloria."

Not bad for a youngster.

"Or someone who is here without us knowing he's here."

Sandra groaned. "Don't say that. And that's not possible. Right after Treasure died, Billy went out and walked all the way around the building. And there were no fresh tracks of anyone coming or going. Whoever pushed Treasure had already been here for a while."

"But someone could have been here before any of us got here," Bob said. "And how do we know Billy was telling the truth?"

Sandra rolled her eyes. "You're an angel. Can't you just flit around the building and peek in all the rooms, make sure there are no stowaways?"

"Good idea. Be right back." He vanished, leaving them stranded in the dark.

"He took our flashlight."

"Hang on." Sandra fished her candle nub and her lighter out of her pockets and tried to light the tired wick.

It wouldn't take, and her thumb was getting sore from turning the lighter's wheel.

"Hurry up, Mom. I don't like this."

"I know, honey. I'm trying."

She didn't even know Bob had returned when he flicked the flashlight on and blinded them both.

"Ah!" Peter cried in surprise.

"Sorry. Didn't mean to leave you stranded. And you were right. There's no one else here."

"Give me that." Sandra snatched the flashlight out of his hand. "What are people going to think if they see a flashlight floating around in midair? They'll think a ghost pushed Treasure down the stairs." She didn't give Bob a chance to answer her. "You saw where everyone is?"

"Yep."

"And is anyone acting like a criminal?"

"No. Well, Matthew is in the bathroom smoking pot, but we'll leave him be. So"—he rubbed his hands together—"what's next? We've got things narrowed down to three names, right?"

"Four," Sandra said. "Just because Frank didn't smell like the soap doesn't mean he didn't wear the costume. This is ridiculous. We need new evidence. We can't figure this thing out based on the smell of cheap soap."

"Why was there an open box of soap in the costume room, anyway?" Peter asked.

"There were *several* open boxes," Bob said. "Irish Spring repels mice."

Sandra didn't know if this was true, but it seemed as good a theory as any. "Bob, you promised to sniff the ladies. So let's go sniff Jan. Even if she didn't lock us in here, she's the one who threw the phone into the forest."

"But she's not the one who hid the phone," Bob said.

"Or maybe she did and then forgot where she put it." Sandra didn't know if this was plausible, but she couldn't think of a theory that wasn't at least a little goofy.

"Let's sniff Gloria first," the angel said. "She's closer."

Chapter 23

Sandra didn't see the point in sniffing Gloria. She wasn't strong enough to drag Peter anywhere, and she wouldn't have left her own children alone. Or maybe she *would* dare to leave her children alone if *she* were the killer, because then there would be no one else to fear. She groaned. She hated second-guessing herself. Maybe they *should* go check on her. "Let's go. They're in the green room." She led the way, and her meager troops followed.

She knocked on the door. "Gloria? Can you let us in?"

"Who is us?"

"Peter and me." Not an entirely accurate roster, but it would do.

"Who screamed?"

Poor Gloria, she was probably scared to death. "It was Jan. She saw a mouse."

After a moment of silence, Sandra heard a scraping sound as someone slid the furniture away from the door. The door opened and Corban stood there holding a hand up to shield his eyes from the light.

"Peter!" Corina cried and came running at him. She leapt at him and threw her arms around his neck. "I'm so glad you're okay!"

Peter blushed and gently peeled her arms off him. "Uh ... thanks ... I'm fine."

Corina turned to peer back into the dark room. "Mum, can I go to the bathroom now that the door's open? Puh-lease? I really have to—"

"Only if Sandra goes with you."

Corina looked up at her with doe eyes. "Please?"

She nodded and then shined her flashlight at Gloria. "Why are you guys sitting in the dark?"

"Our candles burned out," she said matter-of-factly. "I've got a little left, but I blew it out to save it for emergencies."

"Okay. We'll hurry back then. I hate to leave you in the dark at all, but we'll go to the bathroom, and then I'll see if I can find you more candles."

Corina was already headed down the hall, so Sandra hurried to catch up, and did so just as Corina let the restroom door swing shut behind her. Sandra caught it, and then stupidly reached for the light switch. Even as she flicked the switch, she knew what she was doing was pointless—but it wasn't. The lights came on.

"How did you do that?" Corina cried from inside the stall.

Sandra didn't know. She opened the bathroom door and looked out into the hallway, which was as bright as daylight. The furnace roared to life. "The power's back on!"

Corina squealed in excitement. Sandra let the door swing shut again and was staring into the mirror at the dark circles under her eyes when she smelled it again—the scent she would forever associate with theater, death, and Smokey the Bear. She looked down at the sink to see a half-used bar of Irish Spring soap. So it was even less a clue than she thought. Anyone who'd washed their hands might smell like the kidnapper. Case in point, Corina stepped out of the stall and up to the sink to dutifully scrub her hands.

Sandra tried to be patient as Corina did a thorough job degerming herself, and then led the way back to the green room. Nothing seemed as dangerous now that the lights were on. It was amazing what a few light bulbs could accomplish. She opened the door and waited for Corina to step inside before shutting it again.

"It's not her," Bob said, and it took a few seconds for Sandra to figure out what he meant. Oh, right. Gloria didn't smell like a truck stop bathroom. Good for her.

"It's freezing in here," Sandra said.

Gloria shivered. "Hopefully not for long, and if the power company is out fixing lines, then that means that the sand trucks are probably out. I don't see how the power trucks could get anywhere otherwise."

"They are out," Sandra said with an inappropriate amount of sureness. Of course, she knew they were out because Bob had seen them, but she shouldn't have been able to know such a thing. "I mean, you're right, they *must* be out by now."

They were all quiet for a moment, as if each was busy listening for an approaching plow truck. Gloria broke the silence by asking, "Did you ever find the phone?"

"Did we ever!" Peter said before Sandra could shush him.

Gloria's eyes widened. "What does *that* mean?"

"Nothing," Sandra tried. "It was Treasure's phone, so it contained some ..." She coughed, unsure how to proceed.

"Smut?" Gloria guessed.

Heat crept into Sandra's cheeks. She coughed again. "Sort of."

"Pictures of *herself*?" Gloria asked.

I really don't want to talk about this anymore. "Yes. And a friend."

Gloria tipped her head back and laughed. "Let me see."

Sandra wasn't sure how to respond to that.

"Not because I want to see compromising photos of her," Gloria explained, "but I might know the man."

"He's not from here."

"I know, but everyone in this county is related, and I know everyone, so—" She held out her hand expectantly.

Sandra froze. Bob had the phone. She felt it slide into her back pocket, and, trying to act naturally, reached back to pull it back out. She gingerly handed it over, nervous about what was going to happen next. "Why do you know everyone?" she asked slowly.

"I'm a pharmacist." A practiced cell phone user, Gloria took only seconds to locate the offending photos. She gasped and looked up at Sandra. "That's Reynold Goll!"

"Who?" Sandra and Bob asked in unison.

"Otis's son."

Sandra looked at Bob, eyes wide. "Where's Otis?"

"I'll go look." And he was gone.

Chapter 24

"Otis is in the auditorium," Bob's voice calmly declared from an unknown location. "Come up here."

Sandra looked at Peter to see if he'd heard Bob as well, and he obviously had, because he was hurrying toward the door. She didn't like the look on his face. That was too much anger for a ten-year-old. "Slow down, this doesn't mean he's the one who grabbed you."

Peter didn't answer. He just kept trucking toward the stairs.

"Where's he going?" Gloria asked.

"To the auditorium."

Gloria flew out the door, not only leaving her kids behind, but acting as though she'd forgotten all about them.

Sandra gave them what she hoped looked like a kind smile. "You guys might want to stay here. This is almost over. I think." She stepped out into the hallway to see her son about to bound up the stairs. "Hang on, we should get Ethel. She won't want to miss this." Peter ignored her, or maybe didn't hear her. She chose to believe the latter. She stopped outside the prop room door and pounded on it. "Come up to the auditorium. We think it's Otis, and Bob found him up there."

The door flew open. Had she been standing there with her hand on the knob? Ethel blinked in the bright lights, the giant flashlight dangling from her hand. "How long's the power been on?"

"Only a minute. I'll see you up there." She ran for the stairs. Part of her wanted to wait for Ethel. The rest of her wouldn't let that part have its way. By the time she got to the spacious auditorium, Gloria was already shoving the phone in Otis's face, trying to steal Sandra's thunder. "It was you!"

Otis did such a good job of acting innocent that Sandra wondered if he was. His son having a relationship with Treasure didn't make him a murderer.

"Everyone, just calm down," Jan said, surprisingly serene given the circumstances.

Gloria looked at Jan and stuck her arm out toward Otis, a sharp accusing pointer finger quivering at the end of it. "He killed Treasure!"

"I did no such thing!" Otis boomed.

"Why would you say such a horrible thing?" Jan cried.

Gloria wiggled the phone in the air. "You think it's just a coincidence that there are—"

Sandra grabbed Gloria's out-of-control arm and forced it down to her side. "Calm down!" she said with an authority that surprised her. "We don't know anything for sure. Let's just talk this through." Sandra knew she wasn't an interrogation expert, but she was also certain that she could do better than Gloria. She looked around the room. Everyone was present except for Matthew and Ethel. What was taking Ethel so long? Was her head injury more serious than they thought? "Can we all just sit down for a minute?"

Some people sat down. Otis didn't. Neither did Gloria.

Sandra sat anyway, hoping they'd follow suit. "Now, we don't know that Otis is guilty of anything, so let's not jump to conclusions. Like Jan has said all along, Treasure might have just fallen."

Gloria started to argue, but Sandra talked over her. "The reason Gloria is so upset is that there are some photos on Treasure's phone. And while we—"

"I can explain!" Otis cried. "Just because my son had a relationship with her doesn't mean I killed her."

Laughter echoed out from backstage, and everyone turned to look at the empty set. The laughter continued as Matthew wobbled out onto the stage. "You?" He grabbed his belly and laughed some more. "You didn't have a *relationship* with Treasure." His fingers made air quotes as he said the word "relationship." Then he stood there with his hands in the air as if he'd forgotten he'd raised them.

"Not me, you ijit. I said *my son*."

Matthew was no longer laughing or even smiling, but his hands were still up in the air. Because Sandra was staring at him, she didn't realize Jan was approaching Otis.

Suddenly, she was only inches in front of him. "Your son was having an affair with Treasure?" She spoke the words slowly, as if she had trouble pushing them out.

Otis tried to look ashamed and failed. "No, wait, it's not what you think—"

Jan raised her hand as if she was going to slap him. "I covered for you! I believed you! I've been such a fool!" She whirled toward Gloria with her hand still in the air, as if she couldn't decide whom to smack.

"How did you find that phone?" Jan asked as if *Gloria* were on trial and she was the district attorney.

Gloria's gap-mouthed expression made it clear that she had no idea how she'd found that phone.

Peter stepped forward. "I'm really good at climbing up mountains in freezing rain."

Jan clamped her mouth shut and looked at Sandra. "Is that where he was when he was missing?" Still using that same accusing tone, as if she were the only righteous person in the room. She didn't give Sandra a chance to answer her question. "Otis was there when Treasure fell. He told me it was an accident, and I believed him. I didn't say anything because I didn't want to tarnish this theater's reputation. I figured the police would see that it was nothing but an unfortunate accident." She glared at Otis. "I didn't know the creep *had a reason* to kill her! He lied to me, and I fell for it! So much for it being an accident! This poor theater! I was just trying to protect it from scandal." A sudden onset of sobs shook her shoulders. "We've lost money the last four years in a row."

"Oh, Jan," Frank said, using the saddest voice Sandra had ever heard. He walked up to his friend and took her into his arms, his chest muffling the sound of her cries.

The puzzle pieces were starting to coalesce into a picture, but that picture didn't quite make sense. "Jan, why did you hide the phone?"

She mumbled something into Frank's shirt.

"What?" Sandra said.

Frank translated, "She knew it would look suspicious that Otis took it. An accidental death doesn't result in a missing phone. So when she heard it was missing, she wanted to make sure it stayed that way."

"It *was* an accident!" Otis cried. "I was just trying to get the phone away from her. But she wouldn't give it to me! She tried to hit me with a hammer! I'm the victim here—"

"Wait!" Matthew hollered from the stage. "Who was sleeping with Treasure, exactly? You or your son?"

As they each waited for someone else to catch Matthew up, Otis took off running for the front door. At first, Sandra didn't even give chase. Where did he think he was going to go? An old man in an ice storm? But Peter went after him, so then Sandra chased after Peter.

Just as Otis reached the door and was about to push his way outside, out of nowhere a giant flashlight crashed into the back of his head. "Ugh!" He toppled over sideways, and for a second, Sandra feared that Ethel had killed him. But then he got to his feet and stumbled outside, one hand holding the top of his head.

Peter charged out after him. "Come on, Mom! We can stop him!"

Chapter 25

Otis drove a giant quad cab four-wheel-drive Dodge Ram with gargantuan tires. It looked like something a teenage boy would fantasize about, but by the time he was old enough to afford one, would know it would be silly to drive around in such a thing.

Sandra drove a minivan. She *loved* her minivan. It was helping her rear three children, but she didn't think it could compete with Otis's rig.

While Otis backed out through the eighteen inches of snow and ice, Sandra and Peter stood staring at the minivan's miniature tires nearly submerged in snow. The precipitation had stopped, but it had done its damage. She didn't think they could possibly follow him. Then she remembered Gloria's shovel. She turned back toward the theater, where everyone else was huddled inside the open door, watching them. "Gloria!" she hollered. "Where's your shovel?"

"What?" Billy hollered back.

"Gloria has a shovel!" Sandra screamed at the top of her voice, which still wasn't very loud. She wished she had her ref whistle, though, short of tweeting out her message in Morse code, she wasn't sure what good it would do in this situation.

"Shovel!" Peter screamed. He was much louder.

"What?" Billy hollered again. Billy could be loud too.

"Never mind that," Bob said, suddenly appearing beside her. He waved his arm in the air and all the snow that was around her tires flew to either side of their car.

"Whoa," Peter said. "That was awesome." He headed for the van.

"Yeah, well, I can't do it for the whole road, so you're going to have to drive with caution."

Before he'd even finished his sentence, Sandra was in the driver's seat, putting her key in the ignition. "It's okay. The plow truck went through at least once before the snow turned to ice. We might well go off the road, but at least we shouldn't get stuck *in* the road."

Peter climbed into the front seat.

"No, sir, mister! You're not twelve yet. Get in the back."

"You let me before!"

"That was a special occasion!"

"Mom! He's getting away!"

"Get in the back!"

With a dramatic sigh, Peter climbed into the back, and Bob appeared in his place.

"Buckle up," Sandra said to both of them and then eased her van out onto the road, grateful she'd had the foresight to back into her spot when they'd arrived at rehearsal. It seemed as though that arrival had taken place years ago.

"You don't have to do this," Bob said. "You don't have to risk your life to catch him. Everyone in the theater is out of danger now that he's gone. Well, everyone except the two of you."

Sandra glanced in the rearview mirror. "He's right. I never should've let you come, Peter. Sorry, I wasn't thinking." She slowed the van down.

"Mom! I'll be fine. Come on! You're losing him."

She sped up a little, but not much. She didn't want to let him get away, but she wasn't willing to drive faster than thirty-five miles an hour to catch up to him.

"At least he left us a trail," Bob said.

"Yep." His tire tracks were the only tracks on the road. "If he pulls onto another road, we'll certainly know it."

"*Are* there any other roads?" Peter asked.

"Yes, there are some camps up here, and there are old logging roads—"

"Why would he pull onto an old logging road?" The "You're crazy, Mom" was implied.

Sandra didn't like his tone. "Because he's a murderer! And he's trying to get away from us."

Bob laughed. "I doubt he even thinks we're following him." Bob's mirth surprised her. He seemed to really be enjoying this. Maybe she wasn't the only one forming an addiction to sleuthing.

"Good. Let him think he's gotten away." Up ahead, yellow lights flashed through the trees. "Is that a plow?"

Neither of her passengers answered her, but the answer became clear ten seconds later when they came around a corner and there it was: a giant ugly county vehicle hogging the whole road. She yanked the car to the right to get out its way.

"Uh-oh," Peter said, and Bob grabbed the handle over the window.

"It's fine," Sandra said, in complete control of her vehicle. "I know how to drive."

"I never doubted you," the angel said.

Behind the snow plow followed two police cars with flashing blue lights.

"Uh-oh," Bob said.

"They're a little late," Peter said.

"Yes, that too. But I meant uh-oh that Otis's tracks are gone."

Sure enough, Otis's tracks had disappeared. He had obviously swerved to drive on the freshly plowed, sanded, and salted half of the road, and Sandra followed his lead. "That's okay. We'll still get him. Bob, grab my phone. It's in the cup holder. I doubt we have a signal yet, but we really should call the police and tell them the murderer is headed back toward town."

"No, no signal yet."

"Okay, keep checking. You should have one soon. And Peter, keep your eyes peeled for where he might have turned off. I doubt he *will* turn off, but if he does, I don't want to miss it."

"You got it, Mom." Peter turned and pressed his nose against his window.

Chapter 26

"You've got a signal," Bob announced.

Sandra put her foot on the brake, and the van slid to a stop.

"Why are you stopping?" Bob asked, his voice tinged with criticism.

"Because if I go around that corner, the signal will disappear." She took the phone out of his hand and dialed 911 for the second time that evening.

"Hello." She tried to sound pleasant as she identified herself and explained the situation.

The operator sounded confused. "But the victim is still at the theater?"

"Yes, but the killer is heading back toward Plainfield, or he might even already be there. I'm not sure how fast he's—"

"The police still need to go to the crime scene, ma'am."

Sandra swallowed her irritation. "I know that, but they don't *all* have to go there, do they? Especially when the killer is about to get away?"

"How do you know he's the killer?" Her skepticism nearly vibrated the phone.

"Because he admitted it, right before he took off running."

"Oh. All right. I'll send a unit your way. What is your location?"

Sandra told her for the second time, though she had to estimate. Somewhere between the narrow Maple Stream bridge and the Plainfield town line. She started driving as she explained this, knowing she wouldn't be all that heartbroken if she lost the signal now. As she thought might happen, the call turned to fuzz and then to a dead line as the minivan descended into another valley.

"Look!" Bob cried out, pointing out the windshield.

Sandra looked, but she didn't see anything. Did angels have supernatural eyesight along with everything else?

"What is it?" Peter asked.

"I think it's his truck," Bob said quietly.

Sandra slowed, still trying to see whatever it was Bob was accusing of being Otis's truck, and then there it was, in the ditch, on its side. "Oh wow, I hope he's all right."

"That's why I like you, Sandra," Bob said. "Because you genuinely care about people."

The praise made her uncomfortable. She hadn't meant to be sappy about Otis's welfare. He was not a nice man, but she didn't want him dead. "I thought you liked me because I help you on secret sleuthing missions."

"Uh, who called who here?"

Touche. She pulled the minivan over to the side of the road and turned her flashers on. "Now what?" Should they get out? Should they wait for the police? Was Otis even dangerous at this point? She didn't think so. Ethel had almost gotten the best of him. If she could take him out, the three of them should be able to handle him, right? Without waiting for Bob to answer, she slowly climbed out of the van. She pulled the collar of her coat up, grateful for the extra costume-room-layers she'd borrowed. "I think we should stay together," she said loudly, again surprised by the authority in her own voice.

"Good idea. Let's." Bob was suddenly ahead of her, almost to the truck, a supernatural head start that annoyed her. It wasn't fair. Peter, on the other hand, was nearly pressed up against her.

"Do you want to wait in the car, honey?"

"No," he said quickly. "You said we should stay together."

THE SHOWSTOPPER

Honestly, she wasn't sure what the right play was. It might be safer to leave her son in the minivan. Or, it might be safer to just keep driving and get him home to his bed. She sent up a silent prayer for protection and hoped she wasn't being too foolish.

"He's not here." Bob stood on the edge of the road, staring down at the pickup. Sandra, wanting a closer look, slid down into the ditch, almost going onto her butt in the process, and peered in through the windshield. Sure enough, he wasn't in there. She looked around, using her phone for a flashlight, as she'd given the actual flashlight back to Peter. "There!" She pointed to fresh tracks heading into the woods.

"Why would he go into the woods?" Peter asked.

Sandra didn't know. Wasn't he worried about freezing to death? It wasn't sub-zero or anything, but it was below freezing, and the wind chill had to be knocking on dangerous. She didn't know what to do. If she let him go, he might die. If they pursued him, one of them might get hurt. Still, she didn't think this was likely. She looked at the safe minivan parked in the darkness and then she looked at the woods. She hated being indecisive.

"Come on, Mom. Let's go find him. We'll be fine. It's not like he has a gun or anything."

We think. Who knew what he had stashed in that giant truck?

Peter started for the woods, and Sandra grabbed him by the arm. "If we're going, I'm going first."

"Actually"—Bob miraculously appeared in front of them—"*I'll* go first. I've obviously got the best eyesight."

Obviously. Though, he was kind of cheating by being an angel and all. "Okay, let us know if you see anything," Sandra whispered, and then took care to take quiet steps as she walked through the noisy crust on top of the snow.

It was no use. While Bob glided along with near silence, Peter and she sounded like a couple of lumbering Sasquatches.

They walked and walked and Sandra was glad she was in good physical shape. Uphill and down, Otis made a straight beeline through the forest. Whether he had a destination in mind remained to be seen, but he was sure staying on course.

Bob stopped short and held up a hand. Sandra and Peter almost crashed into him as they too came to a halt. "What is it?" she whispered.

"Is Otis a hunter?" Bob asked.

Sandra had no idea.

"Yes," Peter said with certainty.

Bob turned toward them and then stepped so close to Sandra that he made her uncomfortable.

"What is it?" She fought the urge to step back.

"Don't look. We don't want him to know that we know, but he's in a tree stand up ahead."

Now *that* was creepy. She immediately looked.

"Don't look!" Bob snapped.

"Oh stop it. He can't see my eyes from his perch, unless he's got angel eyesight."

"I thought he might be a hunter, because he's acting like he knows these woods."

"He's always bragging about his hunting stories. Fishing too," Peter said. "Sometimes I think he's lying. No one catches that many fish."

"If he throws people down stairs, he probably lies about fishing too," Bob offered.

"So what do we do?" She didn't want to climb a tree.

"I'm not sure. Do you have a signal?"

Sandra checked her phone. "No. But I probably will if we go uphill again." She looked around for a hill, but couldn't see anything beyond the range of her phone's flashlight. "Or maybe I should climb my own tree."

"Can he see us right now?" Peter asked.

THE SHOWSTOPPER

Bob thought for several seconds. "Not sure."

"Can he hear us?" Peter asked in a mouselike voice.

"I don't think so. He's at least a hundred yards ahead of us."

"Maybe we should go back." Peter's voice quavered in fear. Or maybe he was just cold.

Sandra took his hand into her own. His fingers were icy. "Maybe we should." Once again, Sandra was annoyed by her own indecisiveness.

Then they heard a semi-manly shriek followed by a mighty crash from about a hundred yards ahead.

Chapter 27

"Did he just fall out of the tree?" Apparently, Peter found that idea exciting.

"I think ... maybe." Bob was already so far ahead of them that he was out of sight.

Peter took off, and Sandra, much to her dismay, brought up the rear. Hadn't this been *her* investigation in the beginning? She lost sight of Peter, and her heart tightened in panic. "Peter!" she called out, even though that probably wasn't smart given that they were in pursuit of a murderer. "Wait for me!"

Seconds later she realized she'd run out into a clearing and looked up to see both Bob and Peter standing still staring at a small hunting camp. "Is this his?" she said breathless.

"I don't think so." Bob pointed to the cabin. Her phone light followed his pointing, to a giant sign over the door that read, "Welcome to Lewie's Lodge." Who on earth was Lewie? And did it matter? Probably not, as he didn't appear to be home. There was no vehicle in the unplowed driveway and no tracks in the pristine snow. There were no lights on inside or smoke coming out of the chimney. They heard a bang and all turned to see a small shed standing on the edge of the clearing. Then they heard the whine of an engine. At first, Sandra thought it was a chainsaw, and her blood ran cold with fear, but then Otis went whizzing by on an ancient snowmobile. Relief washed over her in a blissful wave. But this relief was quickly replaced by a renewed fear for Otis's safety. He really was trying to freeze to death. She'd never forgive herself if he died trying to get away from her.

"I can keep up with him." Bob disappeared, leaving her and Peter standing in the snow. Despite all their movement, her hands, especially the one clutching the phone, were going numb.

Peter took off for the shed at a full sprint, and Sandra, assuming he was hoping for some warmth from the meager shelter, went after him.

She entered the small space and shone her light around its walls, nearly jumping out of her skin when her light passed a giant moose head jutting out of the wall. "Let's go into the house, Peter. There's probably a wood stove, and maybe some blankets.

"I'm not looking for blankets." He ripped a tarp off a mound near the edge of the shed. "I was looking for this." He looked up at her with wide eyes. "You want to drive?"

Not really. But she sure wasn't going to let him do it.

Trying to hide her trepidation, she approached the relic. Despite having endured many a Maine winter, she had no idea how to drive a snowmobile. She didn't even know how to start one. Pretending she knew what she was doing, she swung one leg over the seat and sat down, almost bouncing off the old plastic as her blue-jeaned rear end realized just how cold that seat was. The key was in the ignition, and she turned it, but nothing happened.

"Watch out, Mom." Peter pushed her right knee out of the way and reached down and grabbed a black plastic handle with both hands. She leaned out of his way as he yanked for all he was worth. The machine beneath her belched, but then went back to silent. Peter let the cord slide back into the machine and then yanked again, grunting this time. The machine roared to life, violently vibrating every cell of her body, but then died.

"Maybe it's not going to work." She wished it wouldn't. What was she going to do with this thing once Peter got it started?

"It'll work. You've got to give it some gas. As soon as it starts, push the throttle—"

"What throttle?" she cried.

He pointed toward a small black button on her handlebar. Desperate to not have her son think she was completely useless, she slapped her hand over the handle and nodded. He yanked again, and as soon as she felt the vibration, she gave it some gas. The engine roared, as did her adrenaline and for a brief second, her pride. But then the snowmobile lurched ahead, narrowly missing the shed wall, and almost throwing Sandra off the back of it. She held on, accidentally tightening her grip with the only hand she had on the sled and giving it even more gas.

Precious seconds later, she realized the error of her ways and took her thumb off the button. The engine sputtered, and she panicked that it was going to stall, so she pushed the button again and gave herself whiplash. At least by now she had the good sense to hang on with two hands, but this was quickly getting old. Maybe she should have let Peter drive.

She hadn't realized Peter had been running after her until he jumped onto the back of the sled, wrapped his hands around her waist, and screamed into her ear, "Go, Mom, go!" Absurdly, this reminded her of the Dr. Seuss book she'd read to Peter seventy thousand times during early childhood. What had it been called? *Oh, the Places You'll Go?* Was that it? She tried to remember as she and her son picked up speed and headed toward the icy trees.

Chapter 28

P *eter really should be wearing a helmet.* Sandra slowed the sled down at this thought.

"He's getting away!" Peter cried so loudly that it hurt her ear.

They knew no such thing, of course. They had no idea where Otis was. They didn't even know where *they* were. The trail had sprawled into a dozen branches since they'd started this escapade, and Sandra was certain they'd lost him. It had snowed less here than it had up in the mountains, and it was difficult to distinguish fresh tracks from old ones. She slowed to a stop and turned to look at her son. "We should go back!" she hollered over the engine.

"What? Why?"

The engine sputtered, and she gave it enough gas to keep it alive. "Because we've lost him, and I don't want to run out of gas in the wilderness." She didn't think she needed to list her other reasons. That she didn't want her son to get frostbite or hypothermia. That winter had just started and there really wasn't enough snow yet for snowmobiling, so these trails were in horrible condition. That her back had never hurt so badly in her life, and she was worried that she'd broken it. That she couldn't feel her face.

Peter dropped his head, but he didn't argue.

She wondered how to turn the sled around in the narrow trail, pretty sure the old girl didn't have reverse. After too much time debating her next move, she realized she had to creep ahead until she found a spot big enough to allow a turnaround. She tried to push the realistic worry that such a spot might not exist out of her mind.

Her frozen thumb pressed the throttle. She was dismayed at how tired the ancient lever made her thumb. She was currently suffering from her first-ever thumb cramp. She crept around a corner and it was a good thing she was creeping, or she would have flattened the angel standing in the middle of the trail.

"We have a problem," Bob announced.

"Just one?"

A normal person wouldn't have been able to hear her over the sled's engine, but it appeared that Bob did. "Otis has fallen through the ice. I can get him out, but I need your help. Follow this trail. I'll meet you there." He was gone again.

Sandra sat there with her jaw slack until the cold made her teeth hurt. Then she sat there with her mouth clamped shut.

"Come on!" Peter urged from behind.

But Sandra was still processing. He'd fallen through the ice? As in on a pond or lake? He'd been stupid enough to drive out onto the ice when it was only mid-December? It hadn't been cold enough for long enough to make that safe. Was he insane? She pressed the accelerator, glad she hadn't turned around yet; it was bad enough trying to do the impossible once. Maybe Otis hadn't known he was driving out onto the ice. Maybe he'd just thought it was a field. But he'd known the woods well enough to find a tree stand, a hunting camp, and a snowmobile, so he probably knew where the lake was.

Before she knew it, she had picked up a scary amount of speed. It didn't matter if the man was crazy or if he had killed Treasure—if Bob thought they could save him from an icy death, then she would do her best. So, she sped along, wondering if the skin on her face was going to survive this, when suddenly she didn't understand what she was looking at.

The trail seemed to end. She applied the brakes, and too late realized that this wasn't the trail's end—it was a hairpin turn to the left. She yanked the sled hard to port and gave the brake all she had.

It wasn't enough. The sled did slow, and it did turn, but before it could find the trail again, her right front track slammed into a tree, sending them toward the ground with dizzying speed. Peter let out a small cry that sounded too far away and then the left side of Sandra's body was slammed into the snow, which didn't offer as much cushion as she hoped. The engine spluttered to a stop, plunging the woods into a silence so complete it was eerie. A horrendous pain spread warmth through Sandra's left leg, which was pinned beneath the snowmobile. *Not good. I need that leg for soccer*. She took inventory of the rest of her body, thanked God that everything else seemed to be in order, and then asked that Peter would be okay as well. Where *was* Peter? Why was he being so quiet? She called out his name.

No answer. Her chest tightened, and it seemed as though her blood itself went cold. She lay her head down in the snow and took a few deep breaths, trying not to panic. Then she called out his name again, and she heard a cry, but it sounded too weak and again, too far away. She had to get to him.

She tried to pull her leg out from under the sled, but it was stuck. "Bob!" she screamed at the sky with a volume she'd never managed before. "Bob!" she screamed again, hardly giving him a chance to answer her first call. Then she realized it might be more effective to just call his boss. So she said, "God, please send Bob, or anyone else, to get his machine off my leg." She waited one second, two, and three, and no one appeared. But she did sense that something was different about her leg. It hurt less. Was it her imagination? Or was she just losing feeling in it? Again she tried to pull her leg out from under the sled, and this time it easily slid free, as if it had never been pinned in the first place.

But she knew that it had. So what had just happened? She slowly pulled herself to her feet. Surely Bob hadn't come to shift the sled a few inches and not paused to say hello? Had God sent someone else? Or had God done it himself? The leg still hurt, but even that was subsiding. She turned around and called out to Peter, who didn't answer. She reached to her pocket for her phone, but it wasn't there. She needed it for its light, but she didn't want to take the time to crawl around on the ground feeling for it. She wanted to find Peter. She headed off the trail and into the trees, calling his name.

Chapter 29

Sandra spent half of her energy praying, a quarter of it trying not to panic, and the final quarter of it straining her eyes to see in the darkness. She called Peter's name and then started to count to ten before calling to him again, so that he would have a chance to answer. But she never got past three. "Peter!" One ... two ... three ... "Peter!" One ... two ... three ... "Peter!"

But he didn't answer.

Suddenly, a light flickered between the trees and she ran toward it calling out to her son. Finally, she heard his faint voice calling back.

"Hold still!" she ordered and then he was in her sights, and relief flowed through her like a warm river. She wrapped her arms around his cold body and hugged him like a vise.

"Mom! It's okay, I'm fine!" He tried to push her off.

She finally let him. "You don't understand." She was breathless. "I couldn't find you. I thought the worse. Are you okay? Are you hurt?"

He laughed. "Mom, I told you, I'm fine. Not hurt at all. I sort of flew off the snowmobile. It was awesome."

"Then why didn't you answer me when I called to you?"

"I did! But you didn't give me a chance to answer. You just kept hollering Peter! Peter! Peter!" He started to pull her away, to her right. "I rolled down a bank, and I had to climb back up it."

"But why did you take so long?"

"Take so long? Mom, we only crashed like one minute ago."

One minute ago? Really? That was the longest minute of her life. She exhaled deeply. "Okay, then let's try to find the sled."

"Mom, are you okay? It's right there." He shone his flashlight to her right, and sure enough, there was the sled, looking so benign, blocking the narrow trail. "I can't wait to tell Dad you flipped a snowmobile over." He snickered. "And then walked off in the wrong direction looking for me. Come on, let's flip it back. Otis is drowning."

Still a bit confused and sneaking up on exhausted, Sandra went to his side to help him flip the sled back over, a task which sounded so easy when he'd first mentioned it.

It wasn't. She grunted and pushed and heaved and hoed and—nothing. Her winter boots, while blessedly warm, didn't have great treads, and she spent most of her gumption slowly running in place. Peter seemed to be faring better. At least his half of the sled was jiggling a little. She squeezed her eyes shut and prayed the same prayer again. "Send help, please."

"I'll pull and you push," Peter said, heading for the back of the sled.

"It will crush you!"

"No it won't. I'm smart enough to get out of the way, Mom." He put his small hands on the top of the sled and pulled them toward him. "Maybe if we get it rocking." He grunted and pulled and then let off and it rolled back toward her, and then he grunted and pulled again. Soon, the sled was indeed rocking until on one of those rocks, it swung past the fulcrum and headed toward Peter, who, true to his promise, scampered out of the way. Sandra had no idea if they'd accomplished the task themselves of if they'd received supernatural help.

She also didn't care. She collapsed onto the seat, breathing hard. "Come on, let's go rescue Otis, if it's not too late." She reached down for the pull-cord. She would start the thing herself this time. She'd relied on the ten-year-old enough lately. Praise be, it roared to life on her first try.

"Mom!" Peter hollered into her ear. He shined his light toward the large indentation the sled had left and there lay her phone she still had fourteen payments on. She was so exhausted she thought about leaving it there, but then slowly started to drag herself off the sled. Too late, though, as Peter was on it. He jumped off the sled, grabbed the phone, and was back on board before she would have even gotten her feet on the ground.

"Thank you." She had never meant those words more. She shoved the phone into her pocket and then she was back on the trail she never wanted to start down in the first place.

But for this leg of the journey, they traveled at a more reasonable pace and never encountered another turn in the trail. A long straightaway spilled them out into an opening that sloped down onto a wide flat plane: *this must be the pond.* She squeezed the brake as Peter jumped off. She wanted to scold him for not waiting for the vehicle to come to a complete stop, but she bit her tongue. She fumbled to get her phone out of her pocket with her frozen-useless fingers, but before she could accomplish this mundane task, a light appeared out on the pond.

"Over here!" Bob called.

With a surge of adrenaline, Sandra jumped off the sled and tried to run toward the water's edge. Her legs weren't in a cooperative mood, however, and Peter grabbed her to keep her from falling. "Is it safe to walk on?" she hollered out to Bob.

"Yes! Hurry! What took you so long? It takes a lot of energy to keep this lit."

He didn't know they'd tipped over, which meant he hadn't helped them, which meant *if* they'd had supernatural help, it had come from someone else. Was there an angel in charge of the ATV trails? She'd ask Bob later, when he wasn't so busy. Squeezing Peter's hand so hard she was probably hurting him, she took a tentative step out onto the ice, and then another. Then she realized what she was doing. "Wait here," she said sternly.

"Sorry, Mom. You can ground me if you need to, but I'm not waiting here."

When did he get so sassy? And so brave? Fine. She didn't have time to argue. She headed for Bob's light and saw that he was standing on the edge of open water. Otis hadn't fallen through the ice so much as he'd driven straight off it into water that hadn't even frozen yet.

Bob shot a hand out toward her. "Stay there. I'll push him up, and you grab him and pull him out."

Pull him out? What did he think she was, He-Man?

She heard the water moving and knelt down at the edge of the thin ice, peering into the dark depths. The ice cracked beneath her, and she prayed for safety. Before she was ready, Otis's head popped up out of the water, and then his shoulders. Peter reached out and grabbed one of his arms, jolting her into action. She grabbed the other, and together they grunted and yanked and pushed themselves back across the ice. They'd almost gotten Otis free from the waist up when Sandra lost her grip and Otis rapidly slid back into the water. Peter didn't let go and he started to slide toward the water's edge.

"No!" Sandra dove for Otis's other arm and caught it just before he went all the way under. She looked at Peter to make sure he was okay, and he appeared to be, so she pulled again on Otis, giving it her all and then some, but he wouldn't budge. Where was Bob? Could he give Otis another shove from beneath? And then he did and Otis surged toward them. They pulled again, skittering backward until a lifeless Otis lay face-down on the ice. The angelic light blinked out, and Sandra found herself frustrated with her angel. He couldn't have waited two more minutes? But then the clouds parted and the moon peeked through, giving her enough light to see Otis, and she felt guilty for her frustration. Repenting under her breath, she tried to be gentle and still speedy as she rolled Otis over.

"He's not breathing!" Peter sounded terrified, and his teeth were chattering.

She stared at Otis's chest. "No, he's not."

Chapter 30

Am I really going to have to put my lips on Otis's mouth? She forced herself not to think about it as she bent over his face. His lips were freezing cold, and her body filled with a cold dread. They were too late. They were terrible people. Well, she was terrible. The angel wasn't a terrible person because he wasn't a person, and she couldn't blame her ten-year-old for her terrible decision making or her terrible snowmobile driving. She took another big breath and then breathed into Otis's lungs. And though she feared it was fruitless, she did it again.

"He moved!" Peter cried.

She lunged backward and stared down at him. Nothing.

"He did! I swear it!"

She didn't believe him. Wishful thinking. A trick of the moonlight. She bent in for another breath, and just as she was inches from his face, Otis coughed, sending a small geyser of pond water into the air. She dodged it, but her joy of his being alive was almost crushed by the horror of this narrow miss. She hurried to roll him onto his side, and he grunted. Another good sign. "Peter! Take my phone out of my pocket." She didn't want to let go of Otis. She felt her phone slide out of her pocket and that spot on her butt grew colder. "Do we have a signal?"

"Hang on." Seconds ticked by. "No, we don't."

"I'll get him on your snowmobile." Bob's voice sounded funny, and she looked up just in time to see him pull some green goo out of his mouth. "I hoped that was a pond, but it was a bog." He shuddered. "Get him back to Lewie's Lodge as fast as you can."

It took her several seconds to remember what Lewie's Lodge was. By the time she figured it out, Bob had scooped Otis up and was halfway back to land. Sandra hurried to follow. "All the way back there? Isn't there somewhere closer?"

"No. I just checked." Bob's clothes were dripping wet.

"Can you get him back to the camp faster than that? I don't know if we'll make it in time."

Bob dropped a floppy Otis onto the sled, and then gave Sandra a grave look. "I am not God. My power is limited. Go. As fast as you can."

Confident that this was a very bad idea, Sandra climbed back onto the sled and turned the key. Bob draped Otis's body over her so that Otis's head lay on her shoulder and his icy hands were in her lap, and she realized that all this time, she hadn't been cold at all. *Now* she was cold. So cold, in fact, that she feared for her safety.

"Now you sit behind him, and hold him on to him," Bob said to Peter. "She's going to drive fast."

She didn't understand the angel's confidence in her.

He yanked on the pull cord and the machine came to life. "Now go!" He slapped the back of the sled like it was a horse, and off she went, slowly at first, and then faster and faster. She could see farther ahead of her now that there was moonlight. Miraculously, she remembered where the turns were, and she slowed for those, but on the straightaways, she really opened up, surprising herself. It wasn't that she was worried about Otis dying. It wasn't even that she was worried about her son getting frostbite, though this was a possibility. She was spurred on by the fact that Otis kept moaning into her ear, and that sound was driving her insane.

When she reached Lewie's small dooryard, she was so unprepared that she almost sped by it. She squeezed the brake and shut the engine off before the sled had even stopped moving. In the moonlight, Bob came toward them from the cabin. Light spilled out after him. Good. The camp wasn't so rustic that they didn't have electricity. "I've got him." Bob wrapped his arms around Otis and heaved him over his shoulder. Limited power or not, the being was strong as a lumberjack. "You get inside. I built a fire."

She doubted that he'd *built* a fire so much as he'd snapped his fingers and the fire had just *been*.

Either way, the warmth of the fire was the most exquisite sensation she'd ever felt, and, totally forgetting about the soaking wet drowning victim, she pulled her son closer to the flames. Bob laid Otis down behind them, and then returned seconds later with a stack of blankets. The cabin wasn't warm by any stretch of the imagination, but it was above freezing, and that felt glorious. Bob stood with his hands on his hips. Sandra noted that angels too had to catch their breath after exertion. "Probably still no signal, right?"

Without much hope, Sandra watched her son pull her phone out of his pocket. His eyes widened. "We have one bar!"

The miracles just kept coming. "Call 911," Sandra said. "Call right now."

Chapter 31

Twenty minutes after Peter ended the 911 call, there was still no sign of paramedics or police. The cabin was finally offering some real warmth, and Otis was sitting up and speaking actual words. His first were, "Thank you."

"You're welcome," Sandra said.

He looked around the cabin. "Thank God for Lewie."

Lewie and *Bob*, Sandra thought. "Yes, thank God for Lewie."

Otis chuckled and shook his head. "You sure are a persistent one."

The odd compliment pleased her, and she wondered if it would be weird to thank him. Would it be impolite not to?

"You were my biggest fear," he muttered, staring at the floor. "I thought, 'If only that soccer ref lady wasn't here, I might be able to get away with it.' I knew you'd caught that drug lord last fall."

She didn't think the man had been a *drug lord*, but she let it go.

"That's why I hid your son." Without looking at Peter, he said, "Sorry, kid. I thought it would distract her." He pulled the blanket tighter around him. "I didn't know it was possible to be this cold."

With the exception of her toes, Sandra wasn't cold anymore, but she hadn't driven Lewie's sled into a bog. She glanced at Bob to see how he was faring. Since he was sitting in a chair and not hugging the fire as they were, she assumed he was doing okay.

"I don't know if I'll ever get warm again." He let out a long sigh. "Not that I deserve to." His voice cracked. "I couldn't stand that woman, it's true, but I swear, I didn't mean to kill her. I just wanted to get that blasted phone away from her, and she tried to hit me with a hammer. It was self-defense."

Doubtful.

"She should have just given me the phone."

"Why was it so important to you? In this day and age, those types of photos are everywhere."

Otis growled. The unexpected sound made the little hairs on the back of her neck stand up, and Peter cast her a worried look. She smiled at her son, trying to convey, *We'll be fine. There's an angel here.*

"She had pictures of my son."

Sandra expected him to elaborate, but he didn't. "And is your son married?"

"Yes."

She still wasn't content. She wanted her curiosity satisfied before the police took over, because after that, she'd have to wait and read the papers just like everyone else. "That seems like a lot of effort to protect your son's marriage—"

"I don't care about his marriage. He's running for office. And he will win." He finally looked up at her. "He will win now, thanks to me."

She wasn't so sure. Would people vote for a murderer's son? And wouldn't the pictures come out in the course of the investigation? Wouldn't the media find out? If Otis's son was much like his father, maybe *she* should tell the media. Then she remembered Otis's dear sweet wife and decided she wouldn't do that. One could hope that the son was more like his mom, although he *did* have an extramarital affair with Treasure Foss—

Bob's head snapped toward the door and then he stood up and hurried to the window. Seconds later, the rest of them heard approaching vehicles. Blue lights flashed into the room, and Peter's shoulders relaxed. She scooted over beside him and kissed him on the cheek.

"Wait! Before they come in here, I have to ask you something." Otis sounded scared.

He should be scared. "Go ahead."

"Who put me on the snowmobile?"

Should she lie? Tell him she'd done it? He wouldn't believe that. She tried to act confused. "What do you mean?"

"I mean," he said through gritted teeth, "I remember someone carrying me to the snowmobile, but there's no one else here."

"I carried you!" Peter blurted out.

Oh great, now her sleuthing career was turning both of them into liars.

Otis scoffed, "You? Impossible!"

Peter's face clouded over. He didn't like being doubted, even when the doubt was founded. "Fine then. Don't believe me."

The door to the cabin opened, and Otis glowered at Sandra. "I know there was someone else there, and since neither of you are wet, I'm assuming that someone else also went into the water after me. I'd sure like to thank that person." There wasn't even a hint of gratitude in his voice.

She leaned toward Otis, glad this was probably the last time she'd ever have to lay eyes on the man. "I promise you. There wasn't another human being around for miles."

Chapter 32

The first cop through the door was her least favorite referee—Dwight Padalecki. "Sandra!" he cried as if they were long lost friends.

She forced a smile and granted him a nod.

Another officer followed him into the small cabin, which was rapidly growing smaller. Officer Long, according to his name tag, looked back through the doorway and beckoned to two paramedics.

"Are you okay?" Dwight's concern surprised her.

Sandra got to her feet and her son followed suit. "We're fine, but Otis here is the one who took a dip. He might not be fine."

Dwight turned and looked down at Otis. "This is the man you're accusing of murder?" His voice dripped with sarcasm. *That* was the Dwight she remembered.

"I'm not accusing him of anything. I'll leave that up to you."

"A-huh." Dwight stared at her as if examining her. Examining her for *what*, she didn't know.

She squirmed under his gaze. One of the paramedics put a blood pressure cuff on Otis, while the other checked Peter's pulse. Sandra stared back at Dwight, trying to will him to question Otis while she was still there.

The male paramedic, whose name tag read "Jordan" asked Otis if he was in any pain.

Otis pulled up the leg of his pants. "My ankle is killing me. I fell out of a tree."

To his credit, Jordan didn't laugh at this admission. "Why were you in a tree?"

Otis jutted his chin out toward Sandra. "I was trying to hide from those nuts, but I dropped my phone, and when I went to catch it, I fell. Also, my lungs hurt, and"—he reached for the top of his head—"I have a huge bump from where some old lady hit me."

Way to go, Ethel.

Dwight was being too quiet.

"Have you been to the theater?" Sandra asked.

He nodded. "What a tragedy." His voice held no emotion. He could have been relaying what movies were playing in town.

Sandra couldn't help herself. "There's a smudge of nail polish on the wall inside of the stairwell's railing. I think it matches her nails. She had a phone with evidence on it. I'm not sure where it ended up. I think Gloria Trembley has it. It's got illicit photos on it, and there's a hammer under the register—"

"I think our forensic-trained police officers can handle collecting the evidence without help from a soccer mom."

She sneered at him. She couldn't help it. "You make it sound as though being a soccer mom is a bad thing. Did you find the phone?"

He didn't answer her and stepped away, signaling that the conversation was over.

But it wasn't. Sandra stepped toward him. "Before she fell, the hammer was on a ledge near the top of the stairs. Otis just told all of us that she tried to hit him with it. If that's true, I'm sure her fingerprints are on it."

Dwight knit his brow together. "*All* of you? Isn't it just you and your son here?"

She flinched, hoping Otis hadn't heard Dwight's question, but he had.

"A man might wonder," Otis said. "Sure seems like there was someone else here, doesn't it?"

"That's what I meant," she hurried to say. "He told the two of us."

The suspicious look on Dwight's face remained, but she didn't care. It wasn't like he was going to figure out there was an angel in the room, and even if he did, that wouldn't be the worst thing in the world.

Bob appeared beside her. "That was close."

She bit her lip.

"I'm going to go."

This news made her sad. She didn't necessarily want to find another dead body anytime soon, but that was the only time she got to hang out with him. "Thanks for your help."

Dwight started. "Wow, um ... you're welcome. But we're just doing our jobs."

She fought not to roll her eyes and as soon as Dwight looked away, she smiled at Bob and gave him a little wave.

"Thanks for inviting me to help. If you need anything else, just holler." And he was gone.

Dwight's partner began to question Otis, and Sandra crept closer to hear, but it was her turn with the paramedic. No, nothing hurt; no, she wasn't having any trouble breathing; no, she wasn't dizzy; no, she didn't need to go to the hospital—

"Yes, you're both going to the hospital," Dwight declared, and motioned toward the door. "It's protocol."

Jordan began ushering her out the door, and she surrendered to the inevitable. She wasn't going to get to hear this conversation. Oh well. It wasn't the end of the world. It wasn't like she didn't know who the killer was. "Goodbye, Otis. I'll check in on your wife." He didn't respond, and she allowed herself to be led back out into the cold and aboard the waiting ambulance, where Peter was already loaded up. The paramedic climbed in behind them and slammed the door. "What about Otis?" she asked.

"The police will bring him in." The vehicle started to move.

"To the hospital? I doubt he's okay. He was in really cold water for several minutes. He wasn't breathing when we first got him out."

He gave her a small smile. "You're so kind to be worried about him. And yes, I heard about how you pulled him out of the water. Pretty incredible, when he's bigger than you are. And he was wearing several layers of clothing." He looked down at her torso. "Come to think of it, you all are."

"The heat in the theater went out with the power, so we all put on costume clothes to warm up. Good thing too, because when Otis took off running, I never thought we'd be riding around on old snowmobiles and playing in a pond."

He chuckled. "Makes sense. But really, he must've weighed a ton. Still impressive that you were able to get him out."

"I helped!"

Jordan gave Peter a bigger smile. "You must have!" He looked toward the windshield. "Must have been a fight or flight thing. Pretty incredible what adrenaline can do when we need it to.

Right. Adrenaline. That was it.

Chapter 33

"Wait, what?" Her husband's eyes were as big as beach balls, and Sandra feared they were going to pop right out of his head.

"I know, I know, I'm sorry." She felt miserable. Nate had every right to be furious with her.

Nate, Sandra, and Peter sat on the living room couch as morning sunlight started to peek through the windows. She and Peter had changed into their pajamas, and Nate had made them hot cocoa. She was desperate for a hot bath followed by soft sheets, but Nate wanted to talk first.

"It's bad enough that you think you're some kind of private eye, but you can't drag our son into it! He could've been hurt!"

"You're right. But I made the best decisions I could as fast as I could. I didn't ask to be in that theater in that situation. But once it happened, I just tried to be as smart as I—"

"Smart?" He raised his voice. He never raised his voice at her. "It was smart to leave Peter alone with Ethel so he could get snatched? It was smart to chase after Otis once he'd left you all perfectly safe behind? It was smart to run into the woods when you found his truck? It was smart to steal a snowmobile when you don't even know how to drive—"

"Dad, stop!" Peter stood up and glared at his father, his empty cocoa cup dangling from one hand.

"It's okay, honey. Your father is right."

"No, he's not!" Puffy-eyed Peter was indignant. Sandra had never seen him so exhausted. "I was perfectly safe the whole time, Dad, because the angel was always there!"

Everything froze. Peter's face made it clear that he didn't even know he'd spilled any beans.

With mouth hanging open, Nate leaned back into the couch cushions and looked at his wife, who quickly looked at her hands.

After the world's longest awkward silence, Nate said, "The angel?"

Peter looked at his mother. "You didn't tell him?"

She didn't respond. She *had* told him. Months ago. But he hadn't believed her.

Peter fell back into the couch. "I'm sorry, Mom. I didn't know it was a secret."

"It wasn't a secret," she said softly.

After another long stretch of quiet, Nate said, "Sandra, I'm not sure what to think. You stopped talking about this delusion, so I thought it had passed. But now you're telling *our son* about your imaginary friend? That's serious. Maybe we should talk to someone professionally."

"He's not imaginary, Dad." Peter sounded exasperated.

Nate didn't look at him. "I understand why you'd believe your mother, but angels don't appear to soccer moms and then help them chase old men through the woods."

She wished people would stop using the phrase "soccer mom" as though it were derogatory. She vowed to wear her T-shirts more proudly and to get a sticker for the minivan—really claim the title.

Peter stood up and stepped in front of his father. Then he knelt in front of him as if he was about to talk to a child. "Dad, *I* saw him too. His name is Bob, and he's awesome."

Nate's eyes ping-ponged between Sandra's and Peter's. "What do you mean you *saw* him?"

"I mean that he's real. I saw him at the theater. He talked to me. Then he's the one who found me in the shed. And he's the one who found the phone. How else could we have ever found that phone in the dark? Then he stole the front seat of the van from me. And he went into the woods. And then"—Peter grew more excited—"he jumped into the pond and pushed Otis to the top. Twice! Because we dropped him the first time. Think about it, Dad. How else could Mom and me have gotten a man out of the pond? Neither of us were even wet, except for our sleeves, because we helped to pull him out."

The color drained from Nate's face. "Oh my goodness."

Sandra gave him a minute to let it all sink in. Then she added, "And remember how bizarre it was that the soccer ref just *happened* to drop his gun so I could get away?"

Nate nodded slowly.

"Yeah, that was Bob too."

More silence. Then, "I don't know what to say."

She scooted closer to him and leaned her head on his shoulder. "You don't have to say anything. But it's been a long night. Maybe we could talk more about this later. The bathtub is calling to me. I can hear it."

He put his hand on her leg. "It can't be true. It just can't." Apparently, he couldn't hear the bathtub calling to her.

Peter frowned. "Dad, you believe in angels, don't you?"

"Of course," Nate said quickly, "but they don't do these things—"

"Yes, they do." Peter stood up. "May I go to bed now?" He was done talking.

Sandra couldn't blame him. She gave Nate a chance to answer, and when he didn't, she granted permission.

Peter was almost to the stairs when he turned back. "Dad, it's weird, but Mom is good at this stuff. I mean, I think it's partly 'cause she has an angel partner, but also, she's good at it. And I promise, I was safe the whole time." Peter used the banister to pull himself up the stairs.

Nate stared at the empty stairs. "We need to tell him not to tell anyone else. They'll think he's nuts."

"I think he knows that, but yes, we'll remind him."

They sat there for a few minutes, watching the room grow brighter.

"So, it's really true?"

"Yep."

"Why am I having so much trouble believing it?"

"Because you're practical and logical and this is new information for you. I didn't believe it either at first."

He looked down at her. "I'm so sorry. I practically accused you of being insane!"

She forced a chuckle so that he wouldn't feel too miserable. "I know. It's okay."

Nate squirmed in his seat. "Can you make him appear right now? So I can see him?"

This time the chuckle was real. "I can't *make* him do anything. He's an angel, not a genie. And no, I don't want to bother him. He's probably exhausted, but if we're ever in danger, I will definitely ask God to send him back. And *if* that happens, I will definitely ask Bob to show himself to you. I don't know if he will. He's not supposed to do that unless it's absolutely necessary, but I will ask him. But right now, I just really want to take a hot bath."

Nate turned his head and lightly kissed her on the temple. His lips felt like feathers. "Sure. You've certainly earned it."

Chapter 34

S andra's family had just settled at the table for supper when her cell phone rang.

"Please ignore that," Nate said. He likely assumed, along with everyone else at the table, except for baby Sammy who was too young to assume anything, that it was reporters calling again. She was a local celebrity again, and her phone had been ringing off the hook.

Two seconds after her phone stopped ringing, his started. The reporters hadn't called Nate yet, and Nate never ignored his phone, so he popped up to answer it.

"Hello? ... Yes ... Yes ... This is his father. ... Are you serious? ... Well, no, I thought ... You know what? Can I talk to my family and then call you right back?" He hung up the phone and sat back down at the table.

Sandra couldn't take the suspense. "What was that?"

He picked up his fork. "*That* was Peter's director, Frank Flamatti. He says the show is still on, and wants Peter to come to rehearsal tomorrow."

"You're kidding," Sandra said.

"I know." Nate picked up his fork and took a bite of pasta.

"Who's going to play Mrs. Walton?" Joanna piped up.

No one answered her.

"I can't believe it," Sandra said.

Nate swallowed. "Me neither." He looked at his son. "Do you even *want* to finish the play? You don't have to. You don't have to go back there—"

"I want to. Definitely." Peter shoved an entire stick of garlic bread into his mouth. Normally, Sandra would've scolded him for that, but she was too distracted by the issue at hand.

Nate looked at Sandra. "What do you think?"

She shrugged. She didn't know what to think. She was still in shock. She understood that the show must go on and all that, but they'd lost two of their actors, and it wasn't like they had understudies. And Sandra was sure that the back stairwell was still an active crime scene. Well, maybe not *sure*. She had no idea how that stuff worked in real life. But pretty sure. "I guess it's up to Peter. If he wants to finish, then I can support that."

"You don't think it will be too traumatic for him?"

"Dad!" Peter rolled his eyes. "It wasn't traumatic!"

Nate narrowed his eyes in skepticism. "It wasn't traumatic to see a dead body and then to be shoved into a shed by someone wearing a grizzly bear costume?"

Joanna's eyes grew wide.

"Not a grizzly bear," Sandra softly corrected for her sake. "It was *Smokey* the Bear."

"Right. That makes it all better." Nate was oblivious to the fact that he was frightening his daughter.

"Why would Smokey be mean to Peter?" Joanna asked, and Nate finally caught on.

"Oh, he wouldn't. They were just playing."

"Maybe we should discuss this later," Sandra said.

"Do we really need to talk about it at all?" Peter asked. "I want to do it. I made a commitment, and I should do it. They already have to find a new Ma and a new Grandpa. We don't want to make them find a new me too."

The kid had a point.

"Okay," Nate said resignedly.

"Okay." Sandra waited a minute and then asked, "Can you call him back?"

Nate raised an eyebrow. "I can't finish dinner first?"

"I'll do it. If I know Frank, he is anxiously waiting for the call." She held her hand out for his phone, even though it would be just as easy to get up and get hers. He handed it to her and she navigated to recent calls, found Frank's home number, and called it.

Predictably, Frank was thrilled with the news. And after he thanked her too many times, he sprang something else on her. "I don't suppose you'd be interested in taking on the role of Ma Spencer?"

She barked out a laugh. "I'm sorry. I'm not laughing at you, but I can't. I've never done any sort of acting. I'd be terrible."

"You've watched her scenes dozens of times. You know the script better than anyone who isn't already in the play. Would you please consider it?" She opened her mouth to say no, but then Frank added, "We're desperate."

For as long as she could remember, Sandra had found it difficult to say no to people. This time would be no different. "I guess I could give it a shot?" Her voice came out squeaky, and Nate's face filled with panic.

"Give what a shot?"

But she didn't answer him. She was too busy listening to Frank thank her again and again. Her stomach rumbled. Maybe it *had* been a mistake not to wait until after supper to take care of this. "Okay, you're quite welcome. I'll let you go now."

"One more thing, Ms. Provost."

Oh dear. What else could there be?

"Do you think your husband might be willing to play Grandpa?"

No way. This time, she was too shocked to laugh. "Uh ... I doubt it. He's really busy with work, and he's not really old enough to be a Grandpa—"

"We can make him look old. I am quite skilled with costuming and makeup." Frank rarely bothered with humility.

"I'm sure you are. I didn't mean to doubt you. I just don't think he can do it."

Nate tapped her on the arm, and she lifted her eyes to meet his. "I'll do it," he mouthed.

She almost fell out of her chair.

"Tell him I'll do it," he said out loud. Then he raised his voice. "I'd be happy to help, Frank!"

"Oh!" Frank cried, and he was off with the thank-yous again.

"Wow, Dad! Thanks!" Peter sprang out of his chair to give his father a hug, something he *never* did without prompting.

"You're welcome." Looking quite pleased, he returned his son's hug.

It took Sandra another two minutes to get Frank off the phone. Then she looked at her husband, who, just when she thought she had him all figured out, continued to surprise her. "What on earth?"

He tipped his head back and laughed. "I've been thinking that we should do something as a family. I spend so much time at work helping other families that sometimes I miss out on my own. And ..." He winked at her. "I don't know who's playing *Mr. Walton*, and I need to keep an eye on him."

Chapter 35

Sandra couldn't believe how hot stage lights were. Underneath her long-sleeved, floor-length dress, and underneath her makeup, she feared she was melting. She was even more worried about her husband, who had been forced to don a stick-on beard. But he wasn't on stage as often as she was, and so spent less time under the heat lamps.

This was the Friday night show, the second of four, and she wasn't sure she had the stamina to do two more. This gig was exhausting. She'd had to pass on two indoor women's soccer games this weekend, and she was sure those would have made her sweat less. She looked down at her hand, where she'd written one of the lines she kept forgetting and then looked up and delivered it to her fake husband on stage. They were in one of the final scenes—the home stretch.

As fake husband delivered his lines to his fake kids, Sandra stared out into the crowd. They'd sold out for all four shows. The place was packed. Not an empty seat in the house. Jan had feared that negative press would ruin them. This was not the case. Business was booming, despite having actors on stage, namely herself, who had no business being there. The eldest Spencer daughter repeated her line while glaring at Sandra. Oops, she'd been woolgathering and had missed her cue. She hurried to deliver her line and, too late, realized she'd delivered the wrong one—a line she'd already said during the first act. Mr. Spencer gave her a broad smile and ad libbed something that sort of smoothed her mistake over, but then no one knew where to go from there. She hurried to sit beside him on the couch, where she was supposed to be for her next line. If no one said anything before then, she would just get things going from that point in the story. But in her haste, she tripped over the hem of the dress that had been altered to fit the much taller Treasure and before she realized what was happening, her face was rapidly heading for the Christmas tree. She reached out to try to stop her fall, but there was nothing to grab, and so her hands raked down through the scratchy branches of the plastic tree that never could have existed during the Great Depression, knocking off each and every Christmas ornament as they went. The plastic red and green ball ornaments rolled toward the edge of the stage and fell off one by one, each hitting the floor with a distinctive *plink*. Collectively, they sounded like sad wind chimes.

When she finally hit the floor, she considered staying there. The play was almost over: couldn't they just close the curtain? But they didn't, and so she started to peel herself off the stage, grateful that at least she hadn't knocked the tree over. Her fake husband rushed to help her up and in his haste, grabbed her with a little too much familiarity and she instinctively jerked away from him and bumped into the tree—and this time, the tree didn't stand so firm. It toppled toward the edge of the stage as if it missed its ornaments and was in a hurry to join them. She reached to grab it, trying to save it from pummeling someone in the front row, and in doing so, almost went with it, but Mr. Spencer grabbed the back of her dress and pulled her back.

At first, Sandra didn't know what the tearing sound was.

A tiny woman in the front row cried out and stuck her cane up into the air to ward off the falling fake fir tree. To Sandra's surprise, the move worked, and the tree glanced off her cane and crashed to the floor without hitting anyone. Then it rolled down the slanting floor until it rested against the stage, rejoined with its ornaments at last.

Sandra heard Jan swear from backstage. There were a few isolated laughs from the audience, but most people maintained their decorum. Sandra had never been so embarrassed in her life and was on the verge of tears. But at least her back was cooling off. Wait. Why *was* her back feeling such a draft?

A terrible idea settled into her mind, and she looked over her shoulder at Mr. Spencer, who was staring at what she now understood to be her bare skin and a bra strap. "How bad is it?" she whispered.

"Pretty bad," he whispered back.

Even though there were several lines still to go, no one was delivering them, so Matthew chose this moment to be a hero. He sauntered out into the middle of their scene and began his monologue that was supposed to close the show. Sandra was so grateful she wanted to kiss him. In this version of the story, his name was Clay Boy, but she still thought of him as John Boy. He ad libbed a little, reminiscing about how embarrassed his mother had been when she'd knocked the tree over on Christmas Eve, and Sandra knew Frank would be furious with him for taking such liberties, but Sandra appreciated his effort.

As he talked, she backed slowly off stage, and managed to make it all the way into the shadows without showing anyone else her bra strap.

Jan appeared out of nowhere and threw a blanket over her shoulders. Oh goodie—it was wool. "You'll need it for curtain call," Jan whispered.

They were still going to make her do curtain call? Who were these sadists? "I'm so sorry, Jan."

"Don't you dare apologize. You're being very brave to do this at all, and you're doing a great job. We're thankful."

Sandra couldn't believe her ears. Jan was being nice to her. Maybe her brief stay in the clink had softened her heart. Rumor had it that the charges against Jan had been dropped, and Sandra hoped that were true. Jan *had* tried to cover up a crime, but her heart had been in the right place. Sort of.

Jan gave her a quick, sweaty hug. "I'm thankful. Frank's thankful. The audience is thankful. You're a hero."

Sandra certainly didn't feel like a hero, but she felt less like a dunce after Jan's kindness. Jan gave her a little push. "Curtain call time. Give 'em a big smile!"

She wobbled out onto the stage and Mr. Spencer grabbed her hand. The crowd roared with applause that she suspected might be motivated by charity. Whatever, she'd take it. As her eyes scanned the audience, they met a familiar pair staring back, and the sight of him cheered her greatly. Perhaps the most enthusiastic applauder of all, Bob sat in the fourth row, beaming at her. Then he stood up, the first to initiate the standing ovation that followed.

Books by Robin Merrill

Wing and a Prayer Mysteries
The Whistle Blower
The Showstopper
The Pinch Runner

Gertrude, Gumshoe Cozy Mystery Series
Introducing Gertrude, Gumshoe
Gertrude, Gumshoe: Murder at Goodwill
Gertrude, Gumshoe and the VardSale Villain
Gertrude, Gumshoe: Slam Is Murder
Gertrude, Gumshoe: Gunslinger City
Gertrude, Gumshoe and the Clearwater Curse

Shelter Trilogy
Shelter
Daniel
Revival

Piercehaven Trilogy
Piercehaven
Windmills
Trespass

ROBIN MERRILL

Standalone Stories
Commack
Grace Space: A Direct Sales Tale

Robin also writes sweet romance as Penelope Spark.

Want the inside scoop?
Visit robinmerrill.com to join
Robin's Readers!

Made in the USA
Coppell, TX
25 May 2020